THE ISLE OF SOUTH KAMUI AND OTHER STORIES

The Isle of South Kamui and Other Stories

THAMES RIVER PRESS
An imprint of Wimbledon Publishing Company Limited (WPC)
Another imprint of WPC is Anthem Press (www.anthempress.com)
First published in the United Kingdom in 2013 by
THAMES RIVER PRESS
75–76 Blackfriars Road
London SE1 8HA

www.thamesriverpress.com

Original title: *Minami Kamuito*
Copyright © Kyotaro Nishimura 1992
Originally published in Japan by Kodansha, Ltd.
English translation copyright © Ginny Tapley Takemori 2013

A CIP record for this book is available from the British Library.

Cover image: Eric Molina 2006

ISBN 978-1-78308-011-3

This title is also available as an eBook.

This book has been selected by the Japanese Literature Publishing Project (JLPP),
an initiative of the Agency for Cultural Affairs of Japan.

THE ISLE
OF SOUTH
KAMUI AND
OTHER
STORIES

KYOTARO NISHIMURA

Translated by Ginny Tapley Takemori

THAMES RIVER PRESS

The Isle of South Kamui

As of olde there be a creed on this isle. Some say it be superstition, but our people have faythe and rejoyce in it. In tyme of sickness or childbirth, when tilling the land or casting our nets, we give offerings unto the oracle and abyde by its divine revelation. Hence peace reigns.

—The Customs of South Kamui

The sun was shining, but there was a strong southwesterly breeze and the sea was choppy and dotted with white surf. The *K Maru*, a small ship under two hundred tons, was unable to land at South Kamui. We were thus compelled to cast anchor off the coast, and a fishing boat from the island came to collect us.

There were just two passengers bound for the island, myself and a middle-aged traveling salesman with an enormous bundle.

A strapping, suntanned youth naked to the waist was at the helm of the fishing boat, which creaked ominously as we rode the waves. Though the island was there before our eyes we did not appear to draw any closer to it. The boat was permeated with the stench of fish and I clung to the side fighting off an urge to throw up, but the salesman looked utterly unperturbed and did his best to strike up a conversation with me.

"This is my third visit to South Kamui, you know. There's nothing here but fresh air and clean sea, and also the women are wonderfully uninhibited. Can't complain about the service. City folks these days talk about free sex and whatnot, but here on this island they've been practicing something of the sort since way back, and they take especially good care of visitors. A veritable 'isle of women,' you might say."

His "nudge nudge, wink wink" type of talk struck me as peculiarly insinuating and offensive. I said nothing, so he probed further: "Are you here on vacation? Getting away from it all is all the rage these days." He was peering at me with his flushed face thrust close to mine. His breath stank of alcohol. I recalled he had been sipping steadily from a whiskey bottle on board the *K Maru*.

"For work," I answered shortly, clutching my chest. I still felt nauseous, but perhaps I could somehow reach the shore without vomiting.

"Work, huh? No kidding!" The salesman laughed in such a way that could equally imply admiration or contempt.

"I'm a doctor," I said, attempting to deflect his gaze. I was annoyed at being considered on a par with the likes of a salesman. "It is most inconvenient for the island to be without medical assistance, so I decided to come."

"You're a doctor? Oh gosh, I *am* sorry." He made a show of striking his head in contrition. It was the sort of gesture typical of a slick salesman, and I began to dislike him even more. No doubt the products he was peddling were fakes. I scowled disapprovingly, but the salesman continued in his overly familiar and clumsy manner to praise me, "I'm really impressed that a young doctor like you would come to such a far-flung island."

I gave a wry smile despite myself. Just a few days earlier I had been similarly commended for going to South Kamui, albeit in rather more elegant language. It was on the occasion of the farewell party held in my honor. My aging professor, overcome with emotion, had said, "It is truly splendid that a young doctor like yourself should demonstrate a spirit of self-sacrifice by going to such a remote island." I listened humbly, but truth be told, my reasons for going to South Kamui were not as lofty as he suggested.

I simply wanted to get away from Tokyo because I had gotten into trouble over a woman. What was more, the woman was associated with some yakuza who had threatened me, so things were getting particularly ugly. My destination, therefore, was not a primary consideration. I would have preferred to go abroad, to somewhere like France or Germany, but I had no money and was not confident of being able to make a living once I got there. It was then that I heard that South Kamui needed a doctor. The salary was good, so I applied. I had vaguely imagined from its name that South Kamui must be an island in the arc of the Kamui Archipelago stretching off the southern coast of Kyushu toward Okinawa. It would not be so bad to live for a while gazing at the blue sea of a coral reef, I thought, but when I looked again at the map after signing the contract, I was shocked. However hard I searched the Kamui Archipelago from north to south, I could not find any island by the name of South Kamui. Nor should I have done. It did actually belong to the archipelago, but was stranded alone in the ocean some two hundred and fifty kilometers to the southeast, as if ostracized by the other islands. Of course there were no flights there, and the ferry from the main island of Kamui apparently took more than ten hours. "Being so isolated and inaccessible, the manners and customs remain little changed from olden times. The living is meager," read the extremely brief entry in the guidebook. It would probably be a folklorist's dream, but for me it felt like being exiled to a place beyond the reach of civilization. I could hardly back out now having already signed the contract, but I was thinking of finding some pretext to return to Tokyo before the two years of the contract were up.

And quite frankly, rocking in a boat stinking of fish with a red-faced middle-aged salesman jabbering away at me, I was already beginning to regret ever having come to this desolate southern island.

The fishing boat finally drew close to the island.

The "port" was actually a small inlet. The seabed was spread with coral, over which the surface of the water was churned into white foam by the incoming tide. We were splashed by spray, but the water was warm. It was the end of April and the days were still chilly in Tokyo, but here it was already summer.

There was a long, narrow concrete wharf where twenty or so islanders had turned out to welcome me. I saw the uniformed figure of a resident police officer, but there were just four men in all and the rest were women. The women wore white singlets with indigo splash-patterned pantaloons, their faces covered with straw hats and cotton towels to protect them from the strong rays of the sun.

"Some welcome party!" the salesman smirked, looking at me. I didn't answer. The feeling of nausea had not yet dissipated, and besides, the women were so sunburned that I could not tell their ages. I did not find them the remotest bit attractive.

The young man at the helm shouted something loudly at the wharf. His accent was so strong I failed to catch his words, but from the way the women laughed shrilly I thought he must have been teasing them.

Four or five of the women caught the end of the rope he threw them and pulled the fishing boat alongside the wharf. They held the rope steady, but jumping up from the rocking boat to the wharf a step higher was surprisingly difficult. The salesman shouldered his large bundle and leaped nimbly up, but I mistook my timing and ended up stumbling awkwardly on the wharf. Seeing this, the women let out a bright peal of laughter that was nevertheless somehow tinged with cruelty.

The young officer hastily took my hand and helped me to my feet.

The women now started hauling the fishing boat ashore. They seemed to enjoy the task. As they pulled on the ropes, they sang a song. I had heard the rhythmical cries of fisherwomen along the Chiba coast as they hauled in the seines, but compared with their rough voices, the singing of these women was extremely slow and leisurely. I could not understand the words. The one thing I did understand, however, was that every time the women sang "*maguhai*—" the young fisherman chuckled. From this I surmised that in the island dialect the word *maguhai* had something or other to do with sex. I remembered the salesman telling me the women here were uninhibited.

The salesman quickly disappeared off somewhere, but for me there started a long drawn-out speech of welcome. A small elderly man, apparently the mayor, bowed low before me and by way of greeting said extremely politely, "We on this remote island welcome you who have done us the favor of coming from Yamato.

We have little here, but we exhort you to please enjoy your stay at your leisure." I had the feeling that I was listening to someone from the ancient Imperial Court. At first I did not understand what he meant by "Yamato," but after it had cropped up a few times I realized that it appeared to refer to the Japanese mainland. It seemed that the elderly residents of this island still used this antiquated name to refer to Japan. In Tokyo, time raced by at an insane pace, but here it probably stood still.

The plump headmaster of the island's primary school gave me an equally formal greeting. One of the remaining men, in late middle-age, was the postmaster, and his welcome speech appeared to demean his own island: "We are very grateful to you for coming to such a place." These three men, four including the police officer, seemed to be the most important, and the fact that all of the island's dignitaries turned out to greet me was evidence of the highest honor. I should perhaps have been thankful to them, but I was fed up with this long drawn out welcome on the wharf. It amounted to a formal ceremony, with the men appearing to vie with each other to give the longest, most courteous speech. It was just the end of April, but it was already unbearably hot. There was no such thing as spring here, and this season was apparently called "young summer," which might sound very pretty, but the sun was beating down and the sweat poured from my armpits.

After about thirty minutes, their speeches finally came to an end and I was shown around the village. The women had finished hauling up the fishing boat, and now trooped after us chattering among themselves in shrill voices. I could not understand their dialect, but I got the impression they were somehow sizing me up. They frequently raised their voices in laughter. I was beginning to get annoyed. Was I going to provide an endless topic of gossip for them?

Walking around the village, I was struck by its destitute appearance. I had been aware that it was an impoverished island with a population of just three hundred and forty-six, but I had not expected it to be this bad. Even compared to the main island of Kamui, the poverty here seemed in another league altogether. All the houses had old-style straw-thatched roofs, and the dry whitish road sounded hollow underfoot. There were no cars to be seen, but instead oxcarts rolled slowly by. The children went around barefoot. In contrast with the indigence of the settlement, the sky was boundlessly clear, and the greenery was deep and rich with enormous sago palms, papayas, and screw pines. Indeed, I got the impression that the vegetation was so lush that the islanders seemed cowed before it.

I was taken to the infirmary on the edge of the village. The sign reading "South Kamui Clinic" was brand new, but the building itself was a musty old wooden structure. Nevertheless, its roof of galvanized sheet iron seemed to confer upon it an air of modernity that stood out amongst all the thatched dwellings. When I went inside, I realized the medical equipment was far from sufficient. It was even less well-equipped than a small private surgery. The mayor apologized profusely for the lack of budget. I told him that I would manage despite the straightened circumstances, whereupon he finally seemed to relax and his deeply wrinkled face broke into a smile.

The women were still there, lined up outside the window looking in at me. The faces of several small children were also peeping in. I commented with an ironic smile that I felt like a caged animal. Just then, a piercing siren rang out and instantly the row of faces outside the window disappeared.

"What on earth is that?" I demanded in shock.

"Today," beamed the mayor, "is the one day in the calendar when the ban is lifted."

"The ban?" I echoed.

This time it was the young officer who explained briskly, "There's a colony here on the island, of a seabird called the Streaked Shearwater. It's a protected species, but on this day alone they are allowed to harvest them. It's quite exciting to watch. Would you like to accompany me? Your welcome party will be held after that."

The mayor and headmaster both urged me to go as well. There was no entertainment to speak of on the island, and today was a major event for which the entire village turned out. It had even been made a special holiday. What with the heat and the lengthy speeches on the wharf, I was feeling fed up and could not summon any enthusiasm, but when pressed further I grudgingly hauled myself to my feet.

Mount Kamui rose almost two hundred meters above sea level, and the Streaked Shearwaters dug their meter-deep nesting burrows on its southern slope. These were the cause of withered tree roots and landslides, which was why this annual cull was permitted. The birds were unable to rise into the air straight from the ground, and had to waddle down the slope to get the momentum to take off. With much hand gesturing, the officer explained such background details as we climbed the mountain path. When speaking to me, he—and indeed all the islanders—used standard Japanese, but the moment they started talking amongst themselves, they spoke in a dialect that I could not understand. They made such a clear distinction that I was left feeling more bewildered than impressed. I could not tell whether they were trying to put me at ease, or whether they were merely underlining the fact that I was an outsider.

Fan palms and date palms grew luxuriantly on either side of the steep path. I was amused by the wild king banana trees which, contrary to its grandiose name, bore fruit that was no bigger than my pinkie. Apparently it didn't taste of much either.

Just before the summit, I turned to see a panorama of the entire island. That was how small it was. The village was huddled in its center. There were no rice paddies due to the fact that the island relied exclusively on rainwater, and possibly also due to the calcareous soil, and I could see only fields of sugar cane and sweet potatoes.

But the ocean surrounding the island was stunning. The muddy brown sea of Tokyo Bay aside, I had always thought that the true color of the ocean was blue, but the expanse of sea before my eyes now was not so much blue as a deep green. Maybe this was what was meant by emerald green. Capping the northern side of the island, the coral reef stretched in a line marked by white surf. Even the breeze blowing up off the ocean seemed as if it was dyed green.

I lit up a cigarette. For no particular reason I recalled my trip to Hong Kong. After my posting to South Kamui had been confirmed, a group of friends from medical school had sent me off to enjoy a recreational break there before starting my period of exile. In hindsight, as Hong Kong was also an island, my friends had probably intended it in jest. But beyond that there was no comparison. In Hong Kong there was everything; here there was nothing. No cinema or bar, much less a bowling alley. They did not even appear to have television. For someone like me, accustomed to seeing a forest of television antennas, this antenna-free landscape was too weird for words.

The only thing going for this island was its natural beauty. But I was bound to grow weary of this before long. I thought of the king bananas I had seen on the way. I couldn't help feeling that the lack of balance displayed by this fruit was symbolic of the island as a whole—of the contrast between its excessive natural beauty and its impoverished way of life.

When we finally reached the summit, we could hear the whoops of excitement coming from the other side. The gentle south-facing slope was wooded with red pines, and it was here that the women and children carrying hoes and shovels had gathered. There were few men; perhaps the others were out fishing. I sat down on a nearby rock to watch the proceedings. Everybody looked as if they were enjoying themselves. Some families were sitting on straw mats spread out on the ground, eating lunch as if they had come on a picnic. The mayor had called it an event, and indeed there was nothing to suggest the savagery of a hunt. Having brought me here, the officer now rolled up his shirtsleeves and joined in. The whoops of excitement continued unabated. I was beginning to think I had been mistaken in perceiving a hint of cruelty in the women's laughter on the wharf. The islanders were poor, but they seemed open and cheerful.

Nearby there was a woman of about thirty and a girl of five or six, possibly her daughter, who had found a Streaked Shearwater nest hidden in the grass and were digging it up with their hoes. Both mother and daughter were intent on their work. Sweat was trickling down the dark, tanned skin of the woman's face. Each time she sank her hoe into the ground, her broad pantalooned hips quivered. She looked sturdy and tough.

Eventually the Streaked Shearwater's head became visible. Its small black eyes darted fearfully around its surroundings. It had a sharp beak, which the woman adroitly avoided as she grabbed its neck in her strong hands and dragged it reluctantly out of its nest. The bird frantically spread its brown wings spanning almost a meter, and let out a shrill squawk, but at that moment the woman braced her legs and with all her strength twisted its neck, her hips again quivering from the effort. Her daughter produced a knife, and the woman used it to slit open the bird's belly. Blood spurted out and stained the surrounding grass and soil dark red. The woman was sweating profusely as, without a word, she deftly cut out the entrails and slung them into the freshly dug hole.

I was enveloped by the sickly smell of blood. It was as if the surrounding air had become permeated with its stench. Their work done, mother and daughter gave a satisfied smile and put the dead bird into a bamboo basket before setting off in search of their next quarry.

The woman's hands were still caked with blood, now drying to a dark red in the strong sun. Once again I was overcome by nausea. The other women were also killing birds, slitting open their bellies with knives, and pulling out their entrails. I knew that was probably the best method for preserving the meat, but I felt increasingly unable to bear the scene unfolding before my eyes. The image of the entire village turning out for an enjoyable picnic was erased from my mind. Being a doctor, I was accustomed to the smell of blood. But then the blood spurting from the birds' slit bellies was entirely different to the blood I had encountered in the operating theater.

The sun was as bright as ever, but my nausea just would not go away.

That evening a welcome party was held for me at the island's only inn.

It was called an inn, but its main business seemed to be that of general store, and provisions brought by boat from the main island were piled up in a dimly-lit earthen floored space, and from the eaves hung a cardboard sign on which was clumsily scrawled, "Just in: bread, soap, cigarettes."

The landlady and a young maid served the feast of Streaked Shearwater washed down with sugar cane liquor. However, the scene from that afternoon flitted before my eyes, and I was utterly unable to touch any of the meat.

True to form, there were long drawn-out welcome speeches from the leading personages, during which cups of sake were exchanged. I disliked this Japanese way of toasting one's health, which from a doctor's point of view was extremely unsanitary. However, as guest of honor I could hardly refuse, and so I grudgingly went along with it.

At some point the traveling salesman, who was staying at the inn, had slipped into the banquet. He seemed to be particularly fond of this island. He slapped the shoulders of the mayor and headmaster and, frequently raising the sake cup to his lips, proclaimed loudly, "This is the best island I have ever been to!" The banquet was becoming increasingly rowdy. Once the salesman began dancing naked, his corpulent belly thrust out, I fled outside to the garden.

I could hear the sound of drums in the dark night. Looking in their direction, I saw the red glow of a fire halfway up the mountain we had climbed that afternoon. There had indeed been a small shrine around there, so perhaps that was the shrine to the island deity. It looked like they were holding an all-night festival to celebrate the day's harvest of Streaked Shearwaters.

Even though night had fallen, the heat still lingered. I was just lighting a cigarette when the salesman called out behind me, "What're you up to out here?" He was in high spirits, and reeked of alcohol. When I replied that I was watching the fire, he smirked. "Arriving on a festival day, it's bound to be a lucky year for you," he said happily. "How about coming up to the shrine with me now? It's quite spectacular."

With a lewd smile, the salesman explained that in the past there had been women *ama* divers on the island, and their customs had been retained in this festival. The women, in the style of the *ama*, bared their breasts and danced as though possessed around the fire.

"It's pitch black. But all the women have great tits," he commented, grinning.

I tried imagining the half-naked women in the light of the fire. It was a healthy, erotic scene that I should have enjoyed, but it just left me cold. It was inextricably connected with the image of the woman slitting the Streaked Shearwater's belly that afternoon.

"The head priest here is known as the 'Chief.' He's a small, feeble old man." The salesman continued his account of the festival. Knowing nothing about the island, I must have been the ideal audience for him. The only reason I was tamely listening to him now was not because I had any interest in the festival itself, but because it was preferable to remaining in that dull banquet with the mayor and the rest of them. "As its name suggests, there is a legend that this island was created by a god. South Kamui's version of Ninigi's heavenly descent, I suppose you could call it. The Chief is descended from the god and is apparently able to hear him speak. He has tremendous authority. In the olden days it seems he had the customary privileges, too. Lucky bastard."

"Customary privileges?"

"Surely you know what that means? He got to sample all the virgins. Although it'd be wasted on an old body like his."

The salesman sniggered and nudged me in the ribs. He was completely absorbed in his own story.

"At the festival, several of the island's youths are chosen to don devil masks and they become the god's messengers. Apparently, if the old Chief ever gave them the order to 'Kill!' they would grab the arms and legs of the person to be sacrificed and mercilessly rip them apart, you know."

His words made me think again of the Streaked Shearwater's white belly slit open by the woman.

"That was long ago, wasn't it? They can't do things like that now, not with the police officer here."

"No, I guess not."

The salesman ran his hand smoothly over his shiny face, flushed red with drink. I got the impression he was almost disappointed that it was a thing of the past.

"How about it? Won't you come up to the shrine with me? Tonight everyone will go crazy with the festivities, and you'll get your pick of the women. All you have to do is put your arm around a woman, like this, and say 'Let's do *maguhai*,' and most times she'll accept. *Magu* is a woman's you-know-what, by the way."

The salesman illustrated his invitation with hand gestures. I had nothing against women. I had thoroughly enjoyed the extraordinarily soft body of the Chinese girl I'd held in my arms in Hong Kong. The women on this island, though, with their sunburned skin and cruel laugh just did not whet my appetite. And I was tired.

I declined, and the salesman set off for the mountain grumbling to himself, probably about what a bad sport I was. It seemed he had stronger nerves than I did.

I did not feel like going back go the party, so I left the inn and went back to the dispensary.

In the back of the dispensary there was a six tatami-mat room that apparently served as a bedroom. I switched on the light, a naked bulb, and lay down fully dressed on the sunbleached tatami. The electricity supply on the island was shut off at eight in the evening, but the hands of my watch indicated that it was nearly nine. An exception was probably being made on account of the festival. Or perhaps it was a special privilege granted to me as the doctor.

It was hot and I dozed fitfully. The monotonous drumbeat was setting my nerves on edge. Drumming at festivals on the mainland was rousing and had a gaiety entirely befitting a festive occasion, but the drums I heard now were dull and cheerless, like dripping rain.

As I turned over, the sound of a cat mewing came from the direction of the dispensary. I hated cats. I tutted to myself, got up, and went down into the dispensary and switched on the light. There under the desk cowered a white kitten.

"Tssss!" I hissed at it, trying to drive it out, but the creature just bared its fangs and made no attempt to move from under the desk. I was beginning to lose my temper. It was not just that I disliked like cats, but rather that everything I had encountered on this island since arriving here today had rubbed me the wrong way. I reached out a hand, grabbed the animal by the scruff of the neck, and roughly threw it outside.

I went back to the other room and lay down. I felt terribly tired. *I don't like this island…*

Muttering this over and over again to myself, I fell into a light doze.

I had no idea how long I had been asleep. When I awoke, I sensed the presence of someone in the room. The electric light had been switched off, and in its place, blue-white moonlight shone in through the open window. Perhaps it was because the air was clearer than in Tokyo, but it felt as though even the night air was tinted blue-white, and although I knew I was awake, I had the strange sensation of still being in a dream.

A woman was standing by the window, and it was only the eerie atmosphere that prevented me from crying out. Feeling that it was a continuation of my dream, I gazed blankly at her. She was very slowly removing her pantaloons. Her upper body was already naked, and her breasts swung heavily in the moonlight. Once she was completely naked, she knelt on the tatami. Finally I was released from the moon's spell and hastily got to my feet. The woman looked as if she was praying with her arms stretched out to me. As she drew her dark, tanned face close to mine, I realized that I had seen her before. It was the woman who had slit open the Streaked Shearwater's belly right in front of me that afternoon.

I had no idea what she was doing here, naked. She sidled up to me and put her arms around my neck and, as if intoning an incantation, said playfully, "It is the god's will." Her dark skin smelled of the sea. She wore a crimson flower in her hair, a southern bloom with a bright, venomous redness. The bittersweet fragrance of its large petals enveloped me.

I tried to break loose, but her muscular arms held fast around my neck.

"It is the god's will." Repeating the same words, the woman pressed her heavy breasts tight against my chest, forcing me down onto the tatami. Her plump, sturdy hips bore down heavily on me. Her skin was damp and clammy.

"I'll show you a thing or two…" She grinned.

Just then, I caught sight of a demon outside the window, his whole body bathed in the blue-white moonlight. He stood staring down at me and the woman.

"Otaki!" the demon called to her, in a low, faltering voice.

"So the god is pleased, huh?" As if spurred on by his voice, the woman pressed her body against me all the harder and started unbuttoning my shirt. I was overwhelmed by her weight, her body odor with a hint of the sea, and the cloying fragrance of the southern flower.

The demon's face disappeared abruptly from the window, but the shock had drained all the energy from my body. Even so, the woman continued to thrust against my private parts and ground her hips with a seriousness that truly befitted serving a god.

I felt as though I had been caught up in a nightmare, but it was two days later that the real nightmare began.

Life on the island was monotonous and dull. And there was also something ominous about it, although I could not put my finger on exactly what. I knew the demon I had seen was just a young man wearing a devil mask, but it still gave me the creeps.

The natural beauty was the island's one saving grace, but the fierce sunlight made me feel dizzy. I did not go out all that much, but my face and arms still smarted with sunburn.

It was almost midday by the time I finally awoke. The strong sunlight dropped white spots up as far as my pillow, promising another hot day.

I got up and went through to the dispensary to find that breakfast was already laid out on my desk. The mayor had taken the trouble of arranging for the woman called Otaki to bring me breakfast, lunch, and dinner.

The dishes were arranged on an old-fashioned black lacquered tray. It was an extravagant feast for an island as destitute as this. The rice was from the mainland, and the miso soup with pork was not made from the local sago palm miso, but from real soybean miso. That alone was probably out of consideration for me, but I did not have much of an appetite.

I ate a little, but soon threw down my chopsticks, left the dispensary, and headed for the seashore. On the beach near the wharf the women, cotton towels covering their hair, were hanging out fish, their bellies split open, to dry in the sun. The smell of fish permeated the small beach.

As they worked, the women sang to a slow rhythm. It was the same song they had been singing as they hauled the fishing boat up the beach when I first arrived on the island. I sometimes heard that song carried on the breeze when I was in the dispensary. The salesman translated the lyrics for me.

C'mon, let's have a ball
Until the strings tying the pantaloons of all the women rip.
C'mon, let's have a ball
Until the strings tying the loincloths of all the men rip.
And when we've finished our work
Let's all enjoy doing *maguhai.*
Yes, let's all revel in doing it.

If I had heard about this song in Tokyo, I would probably have admired its rugged simplicity. At least I would not have found it offensive. But on this island, when I thought about how many more times I was going to be forced to listen to it, the monotonous, melancholy melody grated on my nerves. My urbanized ears were just not on the same wavelength.

I walked past the women to the small inlet from where I could see the coral reef. Two canoes were moored there, one painted red, the other white.

There was nobody around. I could no longer hear the women's singing, perhaps because I was upwind. White wave crests rose like bared teeth over the coral reef some two hundred meters out to sea, but the inlet itself was as calm as a mirror. A breeze blew over the reef, yet standing there motionless I broke out in a sweat. I stripped down to my undershirt and dipped my toes in the water. It felt good. But as I watched a shoal of richly colored tropical fish swim past in the limpid water, I recalled the police officer's warning not to paddle barefoot in the pools or go swimming. There was apparently a highly poisonous fish that had been known to kill people with its sting. For all the natural beauty, it did not strike me as much fun.

I lit up a cigarette, but I suddenly felt a wave of nausea. I hurriedly threw away the cigarette and clamped my hand over my mouth.

Cloudy white spittle stuck to the palm. I washed it off in seawater. Why was the nausea continuing, I wondered.

There was no way I should feel seasick any more. Perhaps the overly strong sun was to blame? Here it was the heat of midsummer. My nerves could also have something to do with it. No doubt that accounted for my lack of appetite, too.

I moistened my handkerchief in seawater and was just wiping my flushed face and arms when I heard a loud voice calling, "Doctor!"

I turned to see the officer racing towards me. Gasping for breath, he said, "Doctor, they've fallen sick."

I tensed, forgetting my nausea. I did not much care for this island, but as long as I was here I had to fulfill my duties as a doctor.

"Who are 'they'?"

"The mayor and the people from the inn."

"What are their symptoms?"

"A touch of diarrhea and a slight fever. They all say they feel unwell."

"Sounds like food poisoning."

"Well, please come," he said before hastening back.

I returned to the dispensary, stuffed some medical supplies in my bag, and headed for the inn.

It was the mayor, the landlady of the inn, and the young serving girl who had fallen ill. I had no idea why the mayor should have taken sick at the inn, but seeing the officer's odd smile I inferred there must be something going on between the mayor and the landlady.

All three patients were presenting practically the same symptoms. They all had a temperature of almost thirty-nine degrees, and the mayor also complained of painful joints, probably due to the fever.

At first I dismissed it as a simple case of food poisoning. The islanders often ate raw fish, so probably that was the cause. But then I discovered red spots on the landlady's breast that were not consistent with this diagnosis. The spots were livid and round, quite unlike hives. Furthermore, if it was hives then it was unthinkable that three people would present the same symptoms all at once.

"Does it itch?" I asked.

"A little," the woman responded in a small voice.

"How did it start?"

"To begin with I felt something awful queasy—"

When she said this, the officer next to her said to me, as if backing up her story, "Come to think of it, the mayor was retching at the washbasin earlier."

Nausea?

I recalled the nausea that had plagued me ever since arriving on the island.

"Can you think of anything you ate that might have been bad?" I asked all three of them, just in case, but they all replied that they could think of nothing.

The mayor suddenly started vomiting at the sink next to his bed. The officer hastily rubbed his back. It seemed his stomach was empty, for all that he vomited was cloudy white sputum.

I examined him again. On his scrawny old chest, I saw the same red spots as on the landlady's breast. I hurriedly brought to mind a number of clinical cases and compared them. I felt a growing sense of unease.

"Do you know what it is, Doctor?" the officer asked me with a worried look.

To put his mind at ease, I told him, "It's probably something they ate. I'll prepare some medicine for them, so please come and collect it later."

I went back to the dispensary for the time being. The sun was blazing down as fiercely as ever, and it was stifling inside the room.

I sank down into the wooden swivel chair, which made an unpleasant grating noise, and cast my eyes over the medical supplies shelf. There was a jumble of bottles of medicine, boxes of bandages, syringes, and suchlike. The medicine log appeared to include just the standard medicines. No doubt they had hastily sent away for supplies from the main island two hundred fifty kilometers away in preparation for my arrival. If what we were dealing with were an infectious disease, however, these medicines would be of no use whatsoever.

Just then I heard a cat mewing. The same white kitten I had seen before had again crawled under the desk. When I stood up from the chair to shoo it away, I was again overcome by powerful nausea.

I rushed to the sink and threw up. All that came out was some cloudy white sputum, the same as that spewed up by the mayor at the inn. It was the same symptom. I felt a sharp pain stab my lower abdomen, as if launching a follow-up attack. I rushed to the toilet and passed a watery stool. Maybe I was imagining things, but my body felt feverish. I took my temperature and it was over thirty-nine degrees.

What on earth could it be? It was clearly not a simple case of food poisoning.

Suddenly I was gripped by an intense sense of dread.

It can't be...

What I had in mind was a contagious disease notifiable by law. It was terrifying even to utter its name. The fact that I was the only doctor on the island, that I had no satisfactory medicines and that we were far from the main island, let alone Tokyo—the sheer number of similarly unfavorable conditions plunged me into a state of panic.

However, I had to confirm it one way or another. That was a doctor's job, and also knowing the truth was the only way to overcome fear.

Once again I looked over the stock of medical supplies. There was only a small microscope of the type you might see in a science class at middle school. I doubted I would be able to detect the pathogenic microorganism with this. Even if I sent saliva and urine samples to Kamui for analysis, it would take ten or more hours just to get there, and even longer to get to Tokyo. The only other method was to test it on an animal.

I glanced at the kitten cowering under the desk. It drew back in alarm, but I used a stick to chase it out and grabbed it by the scruff of its neck. It set up a high-pitched mewling, but I paid it no heed as I bound its four limbs to the desk.

I washed my hands and picked up a syringe. I felt shaky, perhaps because of the fever. Probably the red spots were already appearing on my body too.

I sucked up some of my sputum from the washbasin. The kitten bound to the desk bared its teeth and raised a wail that set my nerves on edge. I dabbed its tender skin with alcohol, and then plunged the needle in. Its body shuddered slightly. After injecting it,

I set it free on the floor. Once again it crawled under the desk and looked up at me with dazed eyes.

Afterwards, there was nothing to do but wait for the reaction. For the time being, I gave the people at the inn some medicine to control diarrhea.

The sun went down with no particular change in the kitten's condition, but in the early hours its movements became increasingly sluggish. I tried giving it some milk, but it made no move to drink it. Even if I prodded it, its response was dull. It just wailed feebly, but made no attempt to move.

Dawn broke and the sun came streaming in. Just as I was inadvertently nodding off, weary from having stayed awake all night, the kitten abruptly started chasing around as if it had gone quite insane. It appeared to have lost its bearings as it dashed haphazardly at the wall, crashed into it, and collapsed in a heap on the floor. It got up again, but its back swayed and saliva drooled from its mouth. It tottered five or six steps more but again collapsed on the floor. It appeared to have no energy for crying and left long trails of cloudy white spittle across the floor.

These were the typical textbook symptoms. A chill ran down my spine. There could be no doubt about it. Soon the kitten's body would lapse into convulsions and it would die.

I took off my shirt and examined my own body. As I expected, vivid red spots had erupted on my chest and abdomen.

I'm done for now.

I chewed my lip at the thought. Suddenly I was startled by a shadowy figure.

The Otaki woman was standing outside the glass door staring at me openmouthed. I hastily put my shirt back on.

She stood looking at me a while longer, but then dropped her gaze and, opening the door, brought in the breakfast tray as usual. She put it down on the desk without a word, bowed to me, and went out.

I turned my gaze to the kitten. It lay there motionless on the floor. I picked it up, but it was already dead.

I took a towel and wiped away the sweat from my body. I glanced at the breakfast, but had absolutely no appetite.

I had just finished disposing of the kitten's body when the officer arrived, weariness showing on his face.

"Two more people have fallen ill. The headmaster and the postmaster."

"It isn't food poisoning. It's a contagious disease."

I felt shaky, and leaned on the desk with my hands to steady myself. The young officer paled.

"Doctor, are you sure?"

"I don't joke about things like this. Take the new cases to the inn immediately, and keep them isolated from everyone else."

I quickly prepared an antiseptic solution before rushing with the officer to the inn.

At any rate, we had to contain the infection. Then we needed a serum, which in the case of this disease had to be injected within at least twenty-four hours of the symptoms appearing. Would it be possible to get hold of the serum in time?

The news of the outbreak of a contagious disease spread through the island in no time. It was abnormally fast. True the island was small, but it also seemed that the islanders had an instinctive awareness of their shared fate.

I used the radio telephone at the post office to contact the hospital on the main island. I got through immediately, but the line crackled with static and I struggled to catch what was being said.

"This is the new doctor at South Kamui, appointed three days ago," I said raising my voice. My head still felt groggy. "I am reporting the outbreak of a contagious disease on the island."

When I said the name of the illness, the doctor on the other end of the line in Kamui responded loudly, "Are you sure?"

"I'm sure. I tested it on an animal and got a positive reaction."

I described in detail the symptoms that had appeared in the kitten. The doctor on the other end listened in silence. "In that case there can be no doubt. But it's strange," he commented.

"What is?"

"This disease is previously unknown in the Kamui Archipelago. What's strange is how on earth it got here. There have been epidemics in Hong Kong and South East Asia recently, but I haven't heard of anyone traveling from there to South Kamui."

"Ah—" I swallowed hard. I had been so shocked by the sudden outbreak of the disease and the fact that I myself had also contracted it that I had not spared a thought for the crucial matter of the origin of the outbreak. I had probably subconsciously resolved not to think about it.

The only possible conclusion was that the disease had been brought to the island by an outsider. And there were just two visitors—myself and the traveling salesman. I could not imagine that the salesman had recently been to Hong Kong or South East Asia. Considering how talkative he was, it was inconceivable that he would not have boasted about his experiences had he traveled abroad recently. That left me, and I had indeed spent time in Hong Kong just before coming here. I had already been feeling nauseous when I transferred from the *K Maru* to the fishing boat. There was no doubt about it: I was responsible for this outbreak. Me, a doctor! I was doubly dismayed.

"Is something wrong?" asked doctor on the other end of the line. The crackle of static continued unabated.

"No, no," I said hurriedly. "Have you got any serum on hand?"

"I'll have a look. Hold on a moment, please," he said.

While I waited for his answer, I wiped the sweat from my forehead with the back of my hand and looked around me. The officer had accompanied me here, but had already returned to the inn out of concern for the others. I was relieved to find myself alone. I did not want anybody to know that I had been the origin of the outbreak. I hardly knew the islanders, and I certainly did not trust them. If they knew that I was responsible for the contagion, there was no knowing what they would do. Apart from that, there was my own pride as a doctor. It was no dishonor for a doctor to have brought in the disease, but the fact was I had decided to inject myself with serum as soon as it arrived without telling anyone else.

The voice on the other end of the line returned. "Following an epidemic in South East Asia last year, we brought some in from the mainland just to be on the safe side. How many cases have you got?"

"Six. How many—?" I could feel the anxiety welling up inside me as I asked.

"Six cases?" He raised his voice slightly. There was a crackle of static. "Oh dear. We only have five doses of the serum here."

"Only five doses?" I was again gripped with panic. It was not so much consternation as sheer terror at the implication for myself of being one dose short. "If we request extra serum from the mainland, how long will that take?"

"At the very fastest, twenty-four hours. We can bring it to Kamui by plane, but from here to South Kamui, ship is the only way. There is no way we can get it to you quicker than twenty-four hours."

That was too long. "It'll be too late by then," I gasped. "You must know that with this illness the serum has to be administered within twenty-four hours of the first symptoms. Twelve hours have already passed."

"Unfortunately there are only five doses."

Another crackle of static set my nerves even more on edge.

"Well, in any case, please send those as quickly as possible," I said.

"Shall we order more from the mainland?"

"Yes, please do. But please don't tell anyone else that there are only five doses. I don't want to spread panic."

"Understood. If you need help, I can come over to provide assistance."

"No," I hastily refused. If a doctor came from the mainland, they would know that I had been the carrier. "As long as we get the serum, I'll be fine on my own. There's no need to worry."

Having said this with unnecessary emphasis, I hung up. When I left the post office, the sun was as dazzling as ever. In the tension I had forgotten the nausea, but now I felt another wave sweep over me.

I was in a dangerous position. When the serum arrived, it would naturally come to light that there was one dose short. So what should I do? As a doctor, I should certainly sacrifice myself and use the serum to save the other five patients. That was a doctor's duty, and especially so since I was responsible for having brought the illness to the island.

But I did not want to die. Life was too precious. Taking responsibility and sacrificing myself in order to save my five patients would doubtless be commendable, but I was not so honorable as that. Apart from anything else, I did not want to die on this godforsaken island.

As I walked to the inn, I mulled over what I could possibly do to save myself.

As I waited for the serum to arrive, I suppressed the intermittent waves of nausea and strove to maintain an outward show of calm. In order to manage this, I secretly injected myself with a stimulant.

If the islanders found out I was ill, they would realize that I was the one who had brought the infection, and that could well lead to my death.

As the news about the contagion spread, the islanders began to gather around the inn. At first I saw a few figures standing there and assumed they must be concerned family members of the five patients. However, their number gradually increased, and by the afternoon almost all the island's three hundred or so inhabitants were there. The elderly, the young, and the children were there. Even a baby came, carried on its mother's back.

They did not shout or cry out, but just silently surrounded the inn. Even after one or two hours had passed, they showed no inclination to leave. A few squatted down, but otherwise the wall of people standing there remained unbroken. There was barely any expression on those uniformly suntanned faces, and I had no idea what they were thinking.

"What the hell are they looking at?" I asked the officer with a frown. Being watched was not exactly pleasant, especially given the weight on my conscience.

"Everyone is worried," he replied.

"But," I glanced at the wall of people, "it's not going to help at all. How about they go home and get on with their usual routine?"

"I don't think anyone feels like doing that. For everyone here, it's as if we all belong to one big family. That's why they are gathering."

The officer's face showed that he thought it was proper for them to do so. The phrase "a shared fate" flitted across the back of my mind. I was being monitored by a large family group of some three hundred people. As I gazed at the thick cordon of people, I realized my own carelessness, and once again felt dismayed.

It was that woman Otaki. When she stood looking at me through the glass door of the dispensary, she must have seen the red spots that had emerged on my body. She also probably saw the cat's dead body. If she had spoken to anyone else about that, then it would certainly have spread amongst all the people gathered here now.

I could not make out Otaki among them. The feeling of unease would not go away. I was gripped by the anxiety that the entire island knew that I was sick too, and the fear that they may know that I was guilty of causing the epidemic. I even began to feel that the people forming the cordon were not worried about the five patients, but were observing me alone. Before coming to the island I had thought the population of three hundred and forty-six was inordinately low, but now that I was surrounded by such a large group of people I felt overwhelmed by them.

As sunset approached, the wind picked up. Just then the ship bringing the serum from the main island finally arrived.

I went with the officer to the wharf to collect it. The islanders followed in droves at a set distance, and watched as I took the box containing the serum. I did not complain to the officer about them again. After all, he was one of them.

As expected, there were only five doses of serum. I stared at the five ampoules in the box and once again thought how this would signify the death of one human being—of someone other than myself, naturally.

The westering sun had become a huge scarlet ball of fire that quivered as it began to sink below the horizon, staining the landscape red as it went down. When I had first arrived on the island the beauty of the setting sun had taken my breath away, but now the same scene was ominous and creepy.

On the way back to the inn, I surreptitiously slipped one of the ampoules of serum into my shirt pocket unseen by the officer. At that moment, I condemned to death one of the patients asleep in the inn, but I tried not to think about that. The sun went down and a cool breeze blew up from the sea, but I was sweating profusely from my forehead.

When we arrived back the inn, the salesman complained of feeling a little nauseous, his eyes fearful like a mouse's. The mayor, the landlady and her maid, the headmaster, the postmaster and now the salesman too had all fallen sick. It was clear that the cause of the infection had been the exchange of sake cups at my welcome party. Eventually the officer would probably fall sick too, but the serum being sent from the mainland would arrive in plenty of time for him and the salesman.

After reassuring the salesman, I hid myself away and injected the serum into my own arm. Simultaneously with the discomfort from the needle, I felt a small but sharp pain in the depths of my being. I shook my head in an attempt to rid myself of it. I was a doctor. If I were to collapse, five more people would probably die. As the only doctor here, surely it was natural I should administer the serum to myself first? I repeated the same self-deluding words over and over like a worn-out record. I knew perfectly well how flawed this logic was. I had secretly administered the serum to myself because life was too dear to me, was all. Now I would probably not die, but could not be sure that I was safe. There was Otaki for one, and then the problem of my own character remained. I was not confident of being able to go through with such wickedness.

I went back to the sick room and, summoning the officer, showed him the box containing just four ampoules.

"I didn't tell you before because I didn't want to alarm you, but they only had four doses of serum on Kamui."

"So we're one short?" He paled and peered into the box.

"That's right," I nodded, averting my eyes from the victims. "I have requested more from the mainland, but it won't arrive in time for those five."

Pointlessly, I glanced at my watch. My nausea had gone. I would not die now. Did I even fully understand what that meant?

"What should we do, Doctor?"

The officer looked as if he was about to burst into tears. Once again, I pointlessly looked at my watch. The distorted image of my face was reflected in the glass.

"I really don't know. There are five patients and just four doses of serum. Please decide who I should administer them to. I can't decide myself."

"Um—"The officer started to say something, and then stopped. He looked forlornly at the patients, and then out of the window. The wall of people was still there.

The inn's lights were on, but the village was in darkness. All of the islanders without exception must be gathered around the inn. They had remained there motionless for several hours already. How much longer would they stay?

Looking bewildered, the officer was sunk in thought. Then, his face pale, he went to the mayor's bedside and started talking to him in a low voice. Probably he intended to ask him for instructions. But how could the mayor decide someone's death? I was convinced he would be unable to reach a decision, and I again resigned myself to the torment of a long wait. In the event, though, it was surprisingly quick. When the officer returned to me, the confused expression had disappeared from his face, which surprised me.

"We have decided to consult the oracle," he told me in a calm voice.

"The oracle?" I was astounded.

"As long as it's the god's will, everyone will be satisfied. It's the best way. It's the *only* way. Any islander should have known that right away, but I was too confused…"

He left the room and walked straight for the wall of people. It looked as though he intended to tell the islanders everything.

I thought of Otaki and felt a stab of panic. If she had told anyone that I was ill, the islanders would probably be suspicious and kick up a fuss. I held my breath and watched them.

As the officer spoke, a ripple of consternation spread in a wave through the wall. Would they stampede the inn and cross-examine me? "But you were ill too, Doctor. What did you do for serum?" If that were to happen, what defense would be left me?

They began to move. But they headed not for the inn, but instead toward the dark form of Mount Kamui.

When the officer returned, I asked him why they had set off toward the mountain.

"They are going to the shrine. They have gone to hear the divine oracle." The constable glanced at the mountain.

"Did you tell them that there isn't enough serum?"

"Yes, I told them. Everyone on this island is part of the same family, you know. So they have the right to know, and it is better that they do know."

Be that as it may, the fact that they had not interrogated me indicated that they did not know that I was ill or that I was responsible for the contagion. Had Otaki not told anyone? But given that everyone on the island shared the same fate, it was inconceivable that she had not spoken of it to her companions. In which case, perhaps she had not seen anything? Perhaps it had been my own doubts and fears that had convinced me I had been seen?

Presently the flames of a bonfire leaped into life on the mountain.

The sound of drumming started. As before, it was monotonous and dreary.

"What are they doing? There's no time for this! We won't save any of them at this rate."

There was an edge to my voice. For me, the task at hand was sheer anguish, and I wanted to get it over with as soon as possible.

But the officer remained unperturbed and said merely, "Let's wait for the oracle."

In the face of such blind faith, there was nothing for it but to keep quiet.

It was absurd to wait for a divine revelation to decide who should die. It was an anachronism. Insane.

However, there was nothing I could do. Not only was I in no position to propose anything, but faced with the ultimate act of condemning a person to death, I simply lost all power of reason. Deciding someone's death by majority decision or drawing lots was outrageous. The person thus condemned could only be the Absolute. And if that was so, then weren't they essentially a god? I could feel my brain growing addled.

I glanced over at the sleeping victims. They were quietly awaiting the verdict. I did not consider their tranquil demeanor either praiseworthy or noble. I found it puzzling and frightening. They must have known that there was not enough serum and that one of them had to die. So why were they waiting so docilely for the oracle? Was their god such an absolute authority for them? What kind of god was it?

I was growing jittery and began pacing the corridor senselessly. The silence of the victims was grating on my nerves. Soon one of them would die. I was the one who would have killed them. I even started to think they knew this and were censuring me, wielding their silence as a weapon.

I could stand it no longer, and yelled at nobody in particular, "Hurry, can't you?"

All of a sudden the sound of the drums ceased.

A hush fell, and I experienced a momentary sensation of the darkness deepening. Out of the midst of the blackness into the pale moonlight emerged a youth wearing a devil mask. It had none of the refinement of a Noh mask, but was roughly hewn and colored with red and green pigments. It was ghastly.

The masked youth halted before the inn. When the officer went out to meet him, he uttered a cry and hurled an arrow to which a note was affixed.

The arrow pierced the earth at the officer's feet. In normal circumstances I would probably have clutched my stomach in mirth at such an overblown ritual, but now it was no laughing matter. I was in the throes of a nightmare.

The masked youth disappeared back into the darkness. The officer smoothed out the slip of paper and showed it to each of the victims in turn. Neither he nor they uttered a word. This, too, appeared to be part of the ritual.

The officer came back to me and said in a low voice, "Please start."

"What was decided?"

Before the officer could respond, the mayor, who was lying closest to us, answered, "I am not needed."

His voice was feeble due to his debilitated state, but it was steady. He was even smiling.

Flustered, I yelled, "This is a crazy way of doing things!"

The mayor merely said, "This is the best way. Everyone can agree, since I myself am convinced." He looked up at me, a smile hovering on his pallid face.

"I find that hard to believe," I said. But even I knew how inadequate those words sounded. Even words on the legality or righteousness of the situation would have sounded hollow in my mind.

"Well, please get on with it," urged the mayor politely.

There was nothing more that I could say. This whole island was insane. Or maybe it was too normal. Mechanically I administered the four doses of serum, omitting the mayor. Nobody said anything. The mayor closed his eyes and started muttering to himself as though in prayer. Once I had finished, I fled from the inn. Death would soon take the mayor's diminutive body. I did not have the courage to watch.

I wanted to return to the dispensary. It would be intolerable unless I could be on my own, drinking. Stealthily I distanced myself from the inn.

However, I had only gone five or six steps when I felt weak at the knees. From out of the darkness the islanders appeared, murmuring, and were once again forming a large cordon around the inn as though to force me back. I retreated and took refuge in the entrance.

Once they had reached the same position as before, they stopped. Why had they gathered again? Had they come to check that the oracle's instructions had been fulfilled? Had they come to sing a requiem for the dying man? If so, they would not have long to wait.

For a while the islanders and I glared at each other. Or rather, I glared at them. I had no idea what they were looking at, or what they were thinking. I found it harder and harder to breathe. At last I turned my back on them and went back into the room.

The mayor's face was already covered with a white cloth. I averted my eyes.

Maybe it would all be over now. I wanted it to be over.

Later that night the salesman fell ill and the officer also started complaining of nausea. The shipment of serum from the mainland arrived the following morning in time to save them.

And that was the end of the outbreak. As I had thought, the exchange of sake cups at the party must have been the origin of the infection.

Two days later, in the evening, the funeral for the deceased mayor was held at the shrine on Mount Kamui.

The run of fine weather came to an end, and a moisture-laden southerly wind rustled the leaves of the sago palms and sugarcane from morning, but as the time for the funeral approached, it started to rain. In the midst of the downpour, four youths wearing devil masks shouldered the mayor's body wrapped in a white sheet and decorated with hibiscus flowers, and, intoning words of prayer, started climbing the path up the mountain. A procession of islanders followed after them bearing pine torches that hissed in the rain.

I watched the long line of torches from the window of the dispensary. I did not feel like joining them. A bonfire was lit at the shrine, and the sound of drumming started. I always found drumming to be a cheerful sound, but since arriving on this island I discovered it could also sound melancholy.

This time, the drumming would probably continue through the night.

The wind also grew stronger, and the rain beat fiercely on the windowpanes. I took a sleeping pill and lay down. I did not think I would be able to sleep without the assistance of medication.

Thanks to the medicine I did manage to get some sleep, but I had an unpleasant dream.

In the dream, the shadowy form of the god condemned me to death. The god shouted, "Kill him!" and I came under attack from youths in devil masks. I ran as if possessed, back to the dispensary and with trembling hands locked the glass door. But the demons chased after me and started hammering on the door. "Come out here! We're going to kill you!" they yelled, and continued pounding on the door. *Pam pam pam!* I awoke to the sound of someone banging on the glass door.

The glass door was making an awful racket. For a brief moment dream and reality were jumbled together, but this was not the continuation of the dream. Somebody really was pounding on the dispensary door.

The dim light of dawn filtered into the room. I went through to the dispensary, and saw the figure of a person silhouetted behind the curtain over the door.

"Who is it?" I asked.

Instead of answering, whoever it was started banging even harder on the door. I tutted and pulled back the curtain to reveal on the other side of the glass the salesman, dripping wet and deathly pale. As I opened the door, he grabbed my arm.

"Doctor, please help me!" he pleaded, his voice quivering.

I had no idea what he was talking about. For the time being, I took him inside and sat him on a chair. He was shivering as if sick.

"Has the illness relapsed?"

"It's not that. They're going to kill me!" he gasped.

I was none the wiser. "They? Who's 'they'?"

"Those guys!"

"Those guys? Are you referring to the islanders?"

"Isn't it obvious? They've gone mad. They've really lost it. They're trying to say that the mayor died because of me."

"Surely not!"

"It's happened before."

"It has?"

"I read it in a book. Once there was a shipwreck that drifted ashore, and some of the crew had smallpox—"

"Yes, I already know about that story. Half of the islanders died of smallpox because of it."

"I'm talking about the bit after that." Twisting and untwisting his fingers, he continued quickly, "The island god ordered revenge, and the islanders ripped the entire crew to bits."

"But that was over a hundred years ago."

"This island hasn't changed a bit in the last hundred years. All the elders call the mainland Yamato, just like they did a century ago, and you've seen for yourself how they all unquestioningly do whatever their mysterious god tells them to do, haven't you?"

Yes, I had seen it. The mayor had accepted the oracle and chosen to die, and the islanders had acquiesced. This island was ruled by the will of the god. In matters of life and death, at least, it was true.

"But even so, why would they kill you?"

"I've seen it."

"What have you seen?"

"I've been up at the shrine. I had a bad premonition, and went to see what was going on. The mayor's funeral already finished last night, but there they were still glued to the shrine, not moving. They're waiting."

"Waiting? For what?"

"They're waiting for the oracle to tell them the name of the person to be held responsible for the mayor's death. They're holding their breath waiting to hear the name of the person they have to rip to pieces. I know who they're going to choose for their sacrificial offering—me. They think this disease was brought in by an outsider. It's just like that shipwreck a hundred years ago. They're going to make me their scapegoat, I know it."

The salesman glanced fearfully at the mountain. The melancholy drumming could still be heard mixed in with the sound of the rain. It told me that nothing had finished. It had been premature to think everything had finished with the end of the epidemic. In fact, it had probably signaled the start of something terrifying.

I was forced to realize that I had mistaken the true nature of what we call "god." The fact was that god was merciless and always demanded a sacrifice. Had the Christian God not demanded that Christ himself be sacrificed? For the god of this island, which had a strong element of shamanism, it was probably even more natural that it would demand a sacrifice in revenge. How come I had not thought things through that far before?

"However," I said, concealing my dismay from the salesman, "there's the officer here, remember? He can't allow them to break the law."

"You mean that policeman? But he's one of them! He's on their side. You saw how he kept quiet and let the mayor die, didn't you? He believes the oracle. That's why—"

His face froze, and he rushed out of the dispensary. I too went out, as if drawn. He stood stock still outside the dispensary listening. Rain was still falling. Sheltering myself from the raindrops with my hands, I asked, "What's the matter?"

"Listen! The drumming is faster than before. That means revenge is at hand," he muttered hoarsely.

The drumming had indeed taken on a tone of urgency.

I looked towards Mount Kamui, and tried to imagine the three hundred-odd islanders waiting patiently in the rain for the oracle. They must all be drenched through. I was more afraid of those devout islanders than I was of any god.

"Doctor, please help me!"

"Help? What can I do?"

"When they come for me, just tell them that I wasn't responsible for spreading that disease."

"And if they don't believe me?"

"You're a doctor. They'll believe you, alright. Please help me! I don't want to die on this island! The ferry will be here in eight days. You only have to keep it up until then. When they come, tell them it wasn't me. I'm begging you!"

I could not bring myself to answer. There were only two outsiders here. If I testified that the salesman was blameless, it would mean that I was admitting my own guilt. How could I be expected to do that? What was more, if this island god was omnipotent and able to see through everything, then I, not the salesman would be chosen as the sacrifice. If that happened, then it wouldn't be the salesman who needed help. I myself was in danger.

The drumming grew faster and faster. As we listened, the blood drained from salesman's face as though he was a prisoner about to be condemned to death. I, too, must have been white as a sheet.

There was a rent in the clouds, and the bright sun shone through once again.

"The drums—" The salesman's voice caught in his throat.

All sound had ceased. It felt as though the entire island was waiting with bated breath.

I desperately wanted to break the silence. I fought back the urge to yell that it was not the salesman who had brought the disease, it was *me*! *I* spread the germs. I wanted to shout it out. These words would be my death sentence, but if the silence had lasted a moment longer I doubt I would have been able to contain them. But just then the oppressive silence was broken by a low murmur that gradually became louder as it drew closer. The islanders were descending the mountain.

The salesman looked at me. I averted my eyes. For a while he stood rooted to the spot, but as the islanders came into view, as if he could not stand the fear, he suddenly yelled, "I don't want to die!" and sprinted off toward the beach.

The islanders drew close to the dispensary. The four masked youths were at the head of the line. Even in the sunlight, the painted masks were ghastly. But the other islanders' faces were hard, as if they too were wearing masks. Perhaps extreme exhaustion had robbed them of expression. Or maybe their faces had been frozen by their sense of mission as executors of the oracle.

They came to a halt before the dispensary and all looked at me, and then looked at the fleeing salesman.

No doubt I should have confessed my crime at that moment. It was *me*. I was the one who killed the mayor. If you need a sacrificial offering, then please take me.

But instead of confessing, I silently turned my gaze to the fleeing salesman and then shrugged, as if in recognition of the difficult situation.

I betrayed the salesman. I betrayed myself. And if there was a god, I betrayed that god in the most cowardly way possible.

It would have been more human to have pointed a finger at the salesman and ordered, "Kill him!" Just shrugging my shoulders, leaving room for the excuse that I had not actually said anything, had been dishonest.

The islanders slowly turned and started off after the salesman. I too followed after them to see what the outcome of my duplicity would be.

The salesman ran, slipping and falling several times in the mud, before cutting across the wharf to the small inlet where the two canoes were moored. He jumped into one and started rowing for all he was worth out to sea.

The small beach was instantly filled with islanders.

A strong wind was blowing off the sea, and the sea foamed white over the coral reef. The salesman was working the oars hard, but his canoe did not appear to be making any headway.

The four masked youths boarded the other canoe. Their movements were slow, but well-practiced and precise.

I watched from a distance as the four youths rowed their canoe out. Each time the red-painted tips of the four oars glinted in the sun, the distance between them and the salesman's canoe closed fast. It was really no contest. It was cat and mouse.

"Stop!" I yelled. But my voice was drowned out by the sound of the waves and the wind. No, I should say that even if it was drowned out by the sound of the waves and the wind, it was just a faint cry to begin with. I had only shouted feebly and I did not move so much as a step.

A rainbow spanned the sky. The sun was so bright it hurt my eyes, and the sea was blue as far as the eye could see. Within that beautiful scenery, one canoe closed on the other and pulled up alongside, just as in a race. I closed my eyes. I heard neither scream nor angry roar. When I opened my eyes again, the sun was shining as before. Just the salesman and the canoe he had been in had disappeared. It felt as though a gaping hole had opened up in the space where he had been until now.

My knees were shaking, and I had to squat down there and then. I would probably have found it easier to bear if I had been greeted with a bloodbath or vision of burning hell. The tranquil scene as if nothing had occurred merely forced me to imagine for myself what must have happened.

The four masked youths slowly steered their canoe back to the inlet. Four masked executioners. They got out of the canoe and, without a word, walked quietly away in the direction of the village. The islanders, too, dispersed in silence.

I was left alone in the inlet.

The ferry arrived eight days later, but I could not bring myself to board it. If I had run away, the burden on me would have been too heavy to bear. Or you could say that whatever remained of my conscience would not allow me to run away.

I stayed for two years on the island working in the dispensary. I had killed two people on this island—and without even getting my own hands dirty. I intended to atone for my sins, although I knew well enough that it was not something that could be pardoned with a mere two years of work.

Life on the island continued as if nothing had happened, peaceful and cheerful—and dull. The men went out fishing on the emerald sea, exposing their tough sunburned skin to the sea breeze. Those four youths who had worn the devil masks were among them, but it was hard to detect any emotional scars on their faces. They had simply been obeying the oracle, so perhaps they did not feel any distress at having killed a human being. Or maybe wearing the mask had released them from any sense of responsibility. Perhaps their usual character had been transformed when they donned the masks. I did not know.

I did not understand the womenfolk any better. The next day they had continued as if nothing had happened, singing the *maguhai* song as they worked, and laughing that light yet somehow cruel laugh of theirs.

The woman called Otaki was, of course, among them. She continued to bring me food as before, and even if our eyes met, no trace of anxiety or censure clouded her sunburned face. I could only think that she had not seen anything, and knew nothing of the fact that I had been ill.

Other than my own anxiety and guilty conscience, order had been utterly restored on the island, and so it remained for the entire two years I was there.

I hardly spoke to the islanders, and made no effort to get close to them. Neither did I go to the shrine.

Only once did I catch sight from afar of the person they called the Chief, the messenger that conveyed the god's words to the people. He was an ordinary old man, small and somewhat hunchbacked. He was wearing a white kimono of a light fabric that resembled an ancient shroud, and white flowers adorned his head. I had no idea what this getup meant, neither did I wish to know. I wanted to forget everything that had anything to do with what had happened.

I kept my mouth shut and did my job as a doctor. In two years, my sole pastime as such was dangling a fishing line in the sea by the coral reef. I had no idea what the islanders thought of me. All I knew is that for them I was just an outsider. And that relationship would not have changed even if I stayed there for ten or twenty years.

Two years passed, and the day came for me to leave the island.

It was sunny, but just like the day I arrived, the wind was strong and white surf foamed over the coral reef.

All of the island dignitaries, from the new mayor down, came to the wharf to see me off, and just as when I arrived they held a long drawn-out farewell ceremony.

"You really did well to endure such a far-flung island for two years," they kept repeating to me. I bowed my head without a word, and climbed aboard the fishing boat that would take me out to the *K Maru*. They knew nothing. They all thought I had stayed here for two years out of my sense of vocation as a doctor.

After the fishing boat had set off toward the *K Maru*, I noticed that the young man rowing was one of the youths who had been wearing a devil's mask. His body was muscular, but his round face was that of an ordinary young man.

As the island gradually receded into the distance, I felt an irresistible urge to talk to him about the incident two years earlier. Perhaps it was a reaction to the two long years of silence, or perhaps I just wanted to confess the truth.

"That time two years ago," I said, deliberately avoiding looking at his face, "you guys sunk the canoe with the salesman in it. Did your god really tell you to kill the salesman? Did you really believe it was the salesman who had brought the disease to the island?"

"It was all the god's will," the young man said in an unperturbed voice. I felt irritated by his unruffled demeanor.

"Does it never occur to you that the god might get things wrong? Have you never thought that you might have killed the wrong man?"

"The god considers the interests of the island. The oracle is never wrong."

He smiled. That beatific expression grated on my nerves. I was seized by a sudden hatred for this man sitting here before me. I found it intolerable that while I had suffered for the past two years, this youth—just like everyone else on the island—had remained entirely unaffected thanks to his unshakeable faith in the god.

"That salesman was innocent." Suddenly I said what had, up till now, been unspeakable. "I know that for sure. Let me tell you why. It's because I myself was responsible for bringing in the disease. I also fell ill, it's just that none of you noticed it; not just you, but that god you believe in didn't notice either. And so you killed that salesman, who hadn't done anything wrong. That god of yours made a mistake."

I knew these words could well prove fatal for me, but at the same time I was hoping that they would pierce his heart. I was sure he would be upset. How would he react? Would he explode with rage? Would he get angry and cast me into the sea, the same way he had killed the salesman?

But the youth did not get angry, and was not even dismayed. Instead, a rather placid smile played on his weather-beaten face.

"Let me tell you something too, Doctor."

"What's that?"

"You never went to the shrine, did you? If you had, you would probably already know."

"What the hell are you talking about?"

"Otaki is the shrine attendant in the service of the god. She knew you were sick. Of course, that means the god also knew it."

I was aghast. So they had known about it all along! "If that's the case, then why wasn't I punished? Why did you kill the salesman, even though he hadn't done anything wrong?"

"The god considers the interests of the island," repeated the youth, as he continued to pull slowly on the oars. "As a doctor, you were necessary to us. The god was well aware of that. But somebody had to be punished. That's the rule, and also it's the right thing to do. If we didn't abide by the rules, then we would not be able to maintain order on the island. Every time that salesman came to the island, he passed off bogus goods on us. So it was inevitable that he should be punished."

"So do you think it was the right thing to do?"

"The oracle was right. As proof of that, you stayed on the island for two more years, Doctor. All that time, we islanders didn't have to worry about getting sick. It was all the god's will." The youth's smile never faltered, his face was full of confidence.

I felt defeated.

As I was climbing aboard the *K Maru*, I lost my balance and fell awkwardly on the ramp, narrowly avoiding a tumble into the sea.

The young fisherman let out a bright peal of laughter that was somehow tinged with cruelty.

A Summer Reverie

Summer was coming to a close.

The sunlight reflecting off the sand was still strong, but the high waves of the dog days were beginning to show. Beyond the horizon, as yet invisible, the wild storms of the typhoon season were steadily approaching.

The beach had emptied of people, and most of the rabble of beach shack bars and cafes had been pulled down, leaving just the remains of the wooden posts on which they had rested. Even the din of city kids partying late into the night at their impromptu camp on the headland at the end of the sandy bay had fallen silent in the past few days. An occasional sports car still turned up, brimming with youngsters who raced around the beach and danced wildly with the car radio blaring at top volume, but they lacked the raw energy of midsummer and looked strangely plaintive. They themselves seemed aware of this and soon hurried away looking bewildered, back to their regular haunts in the city.

The seaside season here on the west coast of Izu was over. At least it was over for the city youth.

But I was still here. I was seventeen.

Mother had been lying under the parasol reading a book for some time now. Mother—no, I hated calling *her* mother. *She* was just "she." She was young—and beautiful. I found her youth and beauty disconcerting.

When my late father first presented her to me and announced they were getting married, I scowled and refused to talk to him for the rest of the day. He thought I was sulking because I was against him remarrying, but it was just that I felt confounded by her beauty. Even after he died at the end of last year, my confusion continued unabated. Or, more to the point, it had grown even worse.

I slowly stood up and, purposely averting my eyes from her, I undressed and went down to the water's edge. In five days' time, my final summer vacation at high school would be over. I would have to go back to Tokyo, where the aftermath of student protests and a tough baseball club training camp awaited me.

I waded into the water up to my ankles and swung my arms in wide circles, flaunting my youth. I was tall, with well-developed muscles. My former classmate Yukibe had once told me, "Wow, what a great body!" Yukibe's real name was Yukiko Kamiki. She had left school after being punished for participating in the student protests. Quite a few other classmates had also left school. Whenever I thought of them I felt guilty of my lifestyle and attitude governed by a "decadent bourgeois mentality." When I was with *her*, though, my thoughts were consumed with her alone. She controlled me.

I started swimming out to sea. I was of course still aware of her. I looked good when I was swimming. I didn't want to look like a poser, though, so I roughed up my style a bit. I deliberately struck the water hard with my arms. Further out the water abruptly chilled, but I continued at a furious pace. I had to keep it up for a hundred meters or so. Even she would be a little awed by that.

When I drew level with the tip of the headland, I stopped swimming and turned round triumphantly.

The parasol was there, but she had disappeared.

Suddenly I felt the strength drain from my body. Swimming so far so hard had been really dumb, like something a manga character would do. Floating on my back and drifting with the waves, I gazed up at the sky reproaching myself. *Crap*, I thought. Feeling hopelessly wretched, I closed my eyes. Out of the blue I recalled meeting Yukibe in Shinjuku just before the start of the summer vacation. She had left home at the same time as school. When I asked Yukibe where she was living now, she laughed and replied that she was living on the streets. She's awesome.

She's fighting against something. But I—

Back on the beach, my thoughts were once again filled with *her*. She had left her book there under the parasol. I picked it up in my wet fingers. I felt a slight thrill, as if I was peeping into a little secret of hers. But then I saw the book she had been so absorbed in was by that awful guy, a friend of my late father who postured as a top novelist although all he wrote was tedious romances that set your teeth on edge. I couldn't stand his novels. And to think that she had been so engrossed in one of those!

I felt furious with both of them and hurled the book into the sea.

When I returned to the villa a while later, a self-important looking bright red sports car was parked outside. I didn't need to see the license number to know who it belonged to. He was here again. I spat loudly, and went round to the bathroom.

As I turned on the shower and started soaping my body, I could hear her laughter rippling from the living room. There was something different from its usual brightness. When we were alone together, just the two of us, she would laugh a lot too, but then it just sounded bright. Now it was clouded with an awareness of the opposite sex. I deliberately made as much noise as I could in the shower.

I got dressed and went through to the living room.

"Was the sea cooling down already?" she asked me. I quickly glanced at both of them before shaking my head.

"No, it wasn't cold at all."

"It's great to be young. So full of energy! How old are you again?" he asked, but I didn't reply.

She replied for me, "He'll be graduating from high school next year, you know," and then turned to me, "Mr. Takeda was watching you."

The novelist ran his slim fingers up through his long hair and, ignoring me, said to her, "I've had terrible writer's block lately. I thought if I could just gaze at the sea, I might get some new ideas, and so I came out here."

"You talk about writer's block, but I really enjoyed your latest novel, *Parting One Rainy Morning.*"

She was praising the book I had just thrown into the sea. He grinned exultantly. I was not amused. Why was she heaping praise on this tedious novelist?

"I focused on adult love in that one. There have been so many rather childish novels lately and I was consciously making a stand against that trend."

Again paying me no attention, he spoke directly to her, drawing her into "adult talk" and blithely excluding me from their conversation. I was indignant. I was already an adult. At least, I thought I understood the adult world. Feigning composure, I went and sat on the couch and, trying not to listen to their conversation, I kept my eyes glued on her. Her face looked somehow different. At first I didn't know what had changed, but after watching her for a while I realized that her makeup was thicker. And she had painted her nails red. Had she made herself up for his sake? I was beginning to feel suffocated. I did my best not to listen to their conversation, but I heard it all the same. I was jealous of her laughing with relish at his bad jokes, and pleased when she failed to laugh right away. Oscillating like this between optimism and despair was wearing me out and I could feel myself sinking into self-loathing.

I got up from the couch and went out through the back door, heading once again for the beach.

The wind was stronger now. The parasol had fallen over in the sand and I went to right it, but then left it as it was and walked toward the headland. As I walked I tried to fill my thoughts with something other than her.

Would the student protests continue even after the summer vacation was over? What was Yukibe doing on the streets? And then in fall there would be the high school baseball tournament in Tokyo, and as a senior I was responsible for making sure we won it for the first time in five years. There were any number of things I had to think about. But even so, I—

I stopped in my tracks. There, by some rock pools was a little girl of about three or four, her blonde hair sparkling in the setting sun. The child looked sweet in her bikini, her belly button sticking out, and for a while I stood gazing vacantly at her. She was intent on catching a small shore-crab as it poked its head out of a small hole in the rocks. Utterly absorbed in her task, she pouted as she cupped her little hands and quickly covered the hole. But the crab was too fast for her as it retreated back inside. She shrugged. For some reason the crab seemed to want to come out of the hole and soon poked its head out again, and again she pouted and tried to catch it. This was repeated over and over again. She put all her energy into it, and on each failure she gave a deep sigh and shrugged her shoulders. Watching the little girl, I felt something refreshing flow through the core of my being, but at the same time my heart ached. I was no longer capable of getting so excited about a simple crab. If I really made an effort I probably could, but just by making that effort I would probably end up feeling disgusted with myself. With *her,* I rejected my immaturity and did my best to appear grown-up, but seeing this little girl I couldn't help feeling lonesome at the fact that I was already too grown-up.

All of a sudden the girl shrieked. The crab had made its escape and was headed my way. I reflexively dropped to my knees and picked it up. With a surprised look the girl glared at me and let out a piercing scream, "*My* crab!"

I looked at the crab writhing in my hands. It had a red shell. Its strangely vivid redness reminded me of *her* red lipstick, her red-painted nails, and his red sports car. He was probably still making her laugh with his grown-up talk. Was she still gazing at him with that coquettish smile? All at once, I hated the crab.

A look of terror flashed across the little girl's face and she started screaming hysterically. Unawares, I had crushed the crab in my hand. Flustered, I apologized. But her face drained of color, and she inched backwards then turned and fled.

I slowly stood up. The crab had fallen from my hand and lay white belly up. Its legs twitched briefly, but soon stopped moving. A wave came and washed away the dead crab's broken pincers.

Even as night fell, he made no move to leave. She, too, was urging him to stay. I could not bear to face him, so, as soon as dinner was over, I went up to my room.

I flung open the window and gazed out at the night sea. The late August breeze already had a chill in it. There was a moon, but the sea was dark and it had set up an eerie moan as if hiding some mysterious secret. I pictured the face of the little blonde girl I had met on the beach in that dark sea. When she had taken fright and screamed, had my face been so hideously contorted that it could scare a child? And when I watched *her* together with him, was my face unappealingly disfigured by jealousy? I could not bear the thought of that. At seventeen, ugliness was the biggest sin of all. For me, there was no meaning in unattractive youth. Youth had to be good-looking.

I am not ugly! I told myself. How could I be? There was an intensity in my eyes, but that was a sign of my youth. I automatically measured myself against that novelist. He was old. Compared to a seventeen-year-old like me, at forty-something he was already ancient. Compared to *her* twenty-eight years, he was ancient. That bright red sports car wasn't suited to him. An old man in a sports car was ludicrous. He was a joke, a clown. I reeled off a string of insults, but instead of enjoying it, I merely felt depressed. The fact that he was a boring old man who drove a sports car that didn't suit him did not necessarily turn me into an awesome young man. What's more, she still seemed to be happily chatting away with him. Every now and then I could hear them laughing. The sound of her giggling in amusement easily crushed any sense of superiority I might have felt.

I slammed the wardrobe door shut and, opening the drawer, took out my father's hunting rifle. The British-made double-barreled weapon was the one thing my father left to me. He had often taken me hunting with him when I was a child. Hunting is a man's sport, he had been fond of saying. I had enjoyed it, too. I found the solid weight of the rifle in my hands mysteriously calming. I did not know why. Maybe I felt cool handling a gun, or perhaps I felt the presence of my dead father in it.

I loaded the rifle and slipped out of the villa with it. I had an irresistible urge to shoot something.

I walked along the dark beach to the tip of the headland. There was nobody around. The wind howled and the waves crashed, but somehow I had an eerie feeling of being immersed in deep silence.

The pine branches and undergrowth on the headland rustled. I planted my feet in the grass and, raising the gun, aimed out into the night sea. It was dark, and I had no idea what I was shooting at. Yukibe had told me harshly that we had to feel murderous against the system. She was probably walking the streets right now looking for an enemy to kill. Yukibe was happy. She had an adversary to fight, but I did not know who or what to shoot. I chewed my lip and, aiming out into the blackness, pulled the trigger.

I felt a slight recoil. For a brief moment, the dark night was split by a blue-white flash.

What had I just shot? Just his ugly potbelly? *Her* beautiful face? The little blonde girl on the beach? Or myself?

That night in my dreams, I shot *her*.

She was naked. Her body was beautiful. That's why, in my dream, I had to shoot her. As she fell, with bright red blood streaming from her white breast, my entire body was pierced by an intense joy. Even after I awoke, the lingering effects of the ecstasy persisted. And I realized that the lower half of my body was wet from having ejaculated. Normally I would have jumped out of bed in confusion, but this morning I stayed with my eyes fixed on the glow of morning sunlight on the ceiling, ruminating on the dream like a cow chewing the cud.

Why had I had a dream like that? I tried to recall passages I had read on Freud's interpretation of dreams. But my memory was hazy, and I was not confident I would be able to come up with a good explanation. All I knew was that in the real world I would never shoot her. There was no way I'd be able to shoot her with the rifle. Even if she were to say that she was going to marry that novelist, for example, if I was going to shoot anyone it would be him.

So why had I shot her in my dream? And why had I felt such an intense joy? Could it be that I harbored a secret desire to rape her? Flustered, I sat up in bed. Suddenly I felt revolted by the dampness in my groin. I grabbed a towel to dry myself and then pulled on my swimming trunks and rushed down to the sea. I wanted to punish my body.

I had thought that nobody was on the beach, but he was standing there looking scruffy in singlet and long underpants.

"Hey, good morning," he said with a convivial smile. "Are you off for a swim at this ungodly hour?"

"Is there any reason why I shouldn't?" I retorted sharply.

"Oh," he said foolishly, in an odd voice. "We *are* in a bad mood, aren't we? But then, you seem to dislike me."

"I don't like people who write novels."

"I see. So it must have been you then, I suppose."

"What was?"

"Who threw my book in the sea. I found it washed up over there a while ago. I'm not going to get upset about it. From an author's point of view, it's an honor to have something you've written thrown into the sea or set fire to or whatever."

"You think so?"

"By the way, I'd like to give you a bit of advice. Will you listen?"

"Nope." I shook my head vigorously, and walked off to the water's edge. Advice? What sort of advice was he going to give me? Like, don't go waving that rifle around? Like, study harder for university entrance exams instead of spending all your time swimming? He was probably feeling all fatherly. Asshole.

I took a run up and dived headfirst into the sea. The water felt colder than it had yesterday morning, but it felt good.

"Hey!" he yelled at the top of his voice. "Don't swim out too far!"

In defiance of his order, I carried on swimming directly out to sea. I was young. I wasn't old like him. I could easily manage a ten-kilometer swim there and back. When I had almost reached the tip of the headland, I took a deep breath and dived down under water. The sea, which at the height of summer had become dirty and had lost its vitality, was now returning to its original blue. A clear blue world enveloped my body. All sounds were muted. My hands fluttered silent and pale before my eyes. It was delightful. I dived down even deeper. But I had been lulled by the pleasantness, and had carelessly forgotten that the sea was still capable of ruthlessness. All at once a current of colder water took hold of my arms and legs. There was a ringing in my ears as my limbs stiffened and stopped moving. I lost my cool. As soon as I floated up to the surface, I shouted loudly for help in the direction of the shore.

He was on the beach looking in my direction. Choking and swallowing water, I called out again and again to him, "Help me!"

He must have heard me shouting. He took two or three steps, but then stopped. Then, to my astonishment, he turned his back. He was going to let me drown! He—

I felt myself drawn into a deep dark void as I lost consciousness. When I came to, I was lying in my own bed. Blankets were piled high on me, but as I came round I started shivering with cold.

I looked up to see *her* pale face peering down at me. For me, the fact that she was there was more of a miracle than having been rescued.

"You've come round," she said with a gentle smile. "Drink this, it'll make you feel better." She offered me some hot milk.

I sat up in bed and drank some. At last I stopped shivering.

"A fishing boat happened to pass by and saved you. No more swimming out so far, right?"

I nodded wordlessly, but deep down I was feeling acutely ashamed. I had wanted so badly for her to see me as a powerful young man, yet I had shown myself up as a pitiful weakling. My only vindication was that the water had been colder than I had expected. Even that wasn't very convincing. In any case, I had been careless and was saved from drowning by a fishing boat. Even my bronzed body had lost its meaning as a symbol of youth, and had ended up looking ridiculous.

"What about Mr. Takeda?" I asked, averting my eyes. He must be feeling disappointed that I had been rescued. I was furious with him, but at the same time I felt deeply grateful that I had not been rescued by him. If he had saved me, I would certainly have felt doubly humiliated before her.

"He's downstairs working on his novel," she said.

"How long is he planning on staying?" I asked reproachfully.

"Well," she said looking doubtful, "until we go back to Tokyo, I guess."

"Didn't he say anything about his book?"

"His book?"

"The book of his that you were reading on the beach, *Parting One Rainy Morning.*"

"Oh, that book."

She put her hands together before her breast and smiled. Just like yesterday, she had painted her nails prettily. She had been doing so ever since he had arrived. I looked away.

"Now that's a funny thing. I thought I had lost it, but it seems it had fallen into the sea. Mr. Takeda fished it out and brought it to me this morning."

She was beaming with delight as if recounting an entertaining anecdote or something. I was taken aback. I had expected him to snitch on me.

"Is that what he told you?"

"Yes. Why, is anything wrong?

"No."

I looked out of the window. He clearly hadn't covered up the matter of the book out of any kindness to me, I thought. It was probably just the capriciousness of a novelist, or perhaps the conceit of having me in his debt. Given what had just happened, it was obvious that he didn't like me. When I had called to him for help, he had turned his back. I would never forget that as long as I lived. Just as I hated him, he also hated me. I knew the reason. It was because she would be free if it wasn't for me. I was in the way of him winning her for himself.

"Would you like another cup of milk?" she asked gently.

When I was feeling a little better, I went down to the living room to find them drinking tea together. Beside him lay some sheets of manuscript paper, but he hadn't written a single line. It was a blatant lie that he had come here looking for inspiration for his next novel.

"You shouldn't be up yet!" She looked at me with big eyes.

"Your mother's right. You should get more rest," he piped up next to her.

I deliberately ignored him and said to her, "I'm better now. I feel like going out for a walk."

"Don't be long. It looks like rain," she said.

I went down to the beach.

It did indeed look as though it would rain. The sun was shining, but heavy black clouds were racing up from the south. A typhoon was probably on the way.

I gazed at the droning sea. It had been my ally until now.

But you betrayed me…

A week before, she had applauded me as I swam out to a small island. The sea had made me look like a hero to her. Yet this time it had severely betrayed me. It had tried to drown me and had made me a miserable loser in her eyes. I would no longer be able to take pride in my youth and strength before her.

It's all your fault, I muttered at the sea.

When I reached the rock pools, I saw that the crab was still lying awkwardly where it had fallen yesterday, its white belly showing. No doubt when I was rescued, I had looked as ungainly as that crab. And no doubt she had seen me lying unconscious in that unseemly state.

I started slipping into depression. I kicked the remains of the crab as hard as I could into the ocean. Startled flies swarmed up from the small, wretched corpse as it landed on the water and sank.

As if on cue, suddenly the sun went in and rain started falling; as I watched, little ripples formed and quickly became a flood of countless rings in the water. The rain fell in large drops like a storm burst. The raindrops hit the sand, throwing it up over my bare feet. The grains of wet sand clung to me. The raindrops stung my face and shoulders. But I remained motionless where I was. I felt a masochistic pleasure at being beaten by the rain. If it was the same sense of defeat, then the harder, the better. I opened my mouth and swallowed the rain as it poured in.

The downpour stopped as quickly as it had started, and the sun came out once again. At the same time, the pleasurable self-torment also vanished, and all I was left with was the pitiful sense of defeat.

I rinsed my feet in the sea and started walking aimlessly toward the headland. Little by little, the clinging sense of defeat turned into a frustrated rage against myself.

Useless!

As I walked, I muttered the same word over and over. *Useless, useless!*

A car was parked at the beginning of the headland. Two guys of about twenty got out when they saw me.

"Do you know any good places for fishing around here?" asked one.

I saw fishing rods on the back seat of the car. But I really couldn't be bothered to answer. I didn't know why. It was probably because I was angry with myself, or perhaps because I was tired after having been beaten by the rain.

As I stood there without answering, the two frowned at each other.

"What a weirdo," said the taller one, scrutinizing my face. His provocative look really got to me. It probably would not normally have bothered me, but with my nerves on edge, his petty attitude rubbed me up the wrong way.

"What's it to you?" I snarled.

He reddened and glared at me. "If it's a fight you're after, I'm up for it," he said in a low, threatening voice. The sun was beating down from the west, and I had the light directly in my eyes. I was getting annoyed. Saying nothing, I stepped forward and abruptly hit the guy in the face. A sharp sound rang out as he staggered and fell beside the car. "Bastard!" With a savage roar, he got up and came swinging furiously at me. His friend stood petrified and watched in dumb amazement.

I went beserk. All my pent-up rage found an outlet as I rained down blows him. His fists slammed into my face and belly. I was bleeding from a split lip, but I felt no pain.

The guy was about the same height as me, but my build was stronger from baseball practice. As we fought dementedly, he suddenly dropped to the floor and stopped moving. His face was covered in blood. I grabbed his collar and hauled him to his feet, then hit him again.

"Stop!" yelled the other guy on the verge of tears. "Stop, please stop! You'll kill him!"

His sobbing brought me to my senses. The savagery that had taken hold of me slowly dissipated.

"You're crazy! He's half dead," he screamed at me as he dragged his unconscious friend into the car. I watched numbly as the car sped away. I felt no sense of triumph. I began to feel even more wretched than before. I had needlessly beaten someone up.

I looked at my own hands covered in blood. Pain swept over me. I wanted there to be another storm to wash away all the blood. Thick rain clouds were still racing fiercely northwards, but no rain fell.

I went back to the villa still covered in blood and got into the shower. The dried blood caked my skin and would not come off. My body was throbbing with pain, but the mental anguish was worse. Why had I gotten into that fight? I recalled the guy's face as he lay there covered in blood, and the voice yelling, "Please stop! You'll kill him!" rang in my ears and would not go away. Why had I hit that guy? I had absolutely nothing against him. Nothing at all had warranted hitting him. But I had hit him anyway. Even after he passed out, I hit him again. There was no sense of accomplishment or exhilaration at winning. Yukibe would probably laugh at my behavior and say it was nonsensical. I deserved to be laughed at. I was a worthless human being.

I wanted someone to comfort me. I didn't need words. It would be enough for someone to silently watch over me as I grappled with my own wretchedness. Anybody would do. No, that was a lie. I wanted her to comfort me. Nobody else would do.

I tiptoed down and peeked into the living room. She lay on the sofa with her eyes shut. He wasn't there. The fact that she was alone struck me as a miracle.

I went up to the sofa. She had her hands folded on her breast, and was breathing lightly in her sleep. Her sleeping face was beautiful and sensual.

I'm in love with her.

Since she was asleep, I could be honest about my feelings. I was in love with her.

I knelt down and there before my eyes was her face, her breast, alive. What long eyelashes she had! Such white skin!

I touched my lips to the back of her hand, which was folded on her breast. She was so cold! She carried on sleeping unawares. That emboldened me, and I grew more daring. Timidly I touched her slightly parted lips. A sweet fragrance enveloped me and a stab of ecstasy pierced my chest. I had kissed Yukibe sometime or other, but I had merely felt embarrassed. But this was different. My body trembled with joy. I forgot all about almost drowning, about my meaningless fight. My consciousness had been taken over by just one fact. I had kissed *her*. I had *kissed her*!

When I looked up, I noticed a single small spot vivid against her white bosom. It was my blood. When I touched my lips to her, blood had fallen from my wound onto her breast. A moment of panic strangely dissipated as I stared at the spot of red blood. It was stunningly red. It was beautiful. I remembered the dream I had the night before. In the dream, when I fired, her naked white body had been stained red. I was seized by the sweet illusion that the dream had come true. Furthermore, this was my blood. My blood was staining her breast red. A desire to color her breast bright red swept over me. I went to touch her lips again. But just then, with a jolt I felt someone's presence in the room.

I turned around to see him standing in the doorway watching me. I disliked him, but until that moment I had not thought of him as hateful.

I went over to him and fixed him with a glare, "Do you want something?" He smiled oddly, and said, "You shouldn't do that" in a warning tone. "You shouldn't do that sort of thing to her. You'll just get hurt. You're seventeen—it's normal to start liking women at that age, but not *her*."

"Don't talk about her like that!" I yelled.

My heart felt heavy with anger and sadness at having been witnessed by such a man. The blend of anger and sadness was making me feel ferocious. She belonged to me! She was not his.

"But she's your mother. And what's more, she—"

He continued talking in a hoarse voice, still with that unpleasant smile.

"Shut up. *Shut up!*" I yelled, and hit his face as hard as I could. On the headland I had beaten up a man towards whom I felt absolutely no anger or hatred. But now I hit him with the full force of my loathing.

His skinny frame flew back against the window. The glass shattered with a tremendous crash. A shard pierced his arm, and I saw blood spurt out.

"Stop this idiocy now!" he screamed. I paid no attention, and grabbing his shirt I shoved him up against the wall, banging his head against it with dull thuds.

"Stop that!" I heard her voice behind me. As if repelled, I let go of him.

Glaring at me with fierce eyes, she went over to him and helped him up.

"What do you think you're doing?" she demanded accusingly.

Consumed with fierce jealousy, I stared at her as she gently stroked his forehead and cheeks.

"Shinichi and I were just play boxing," he said, puckering his cheeks. So, did he mean to cover up for me? I felt so humiliated, I wanted to throw up.

"Well it's going too far." She took out her handkerchief and dabbed at the stream of blood on his arm. The fulfilment of a moment ago, when I had touched her lips and felt she was at last mine, had been swept away without trace. So it had been nothing more than a momentary illusion after all.

Was that really all it was?

I looked for the spot of blood on her breast. That vivid red spot of blood was the proof that in that moment she and I had been one. It had been a reality, not a dream.

It was still there, but it had already dried up, and had lost the beauty of that moment. Instead, blood from his arm was staining her breast and dress.

"Get me a bandage, would you?" she said, as if she was ordering me. I bit my lip and ran out of the room. Get a bandage for him? You must be joking!

I fled to the twilight beach.

The sky was dark, and the sea surging. The breeze, too, was cold. The empty beach reflected in my eyes was as bleak as a desert.

Subconsciously I was searching for the little blonde girl, her hair glinting in the rays of the setting sun, her cute pouting mouth, and her small hands. I wanted to see her again. It would be enough just to see her. If I could just see her cute figure and serious eyes, perhaps I could get some respite from this crushing sense of despair.

I carried on walking along the beach.

The rain started with a thunderous roar, like a horse abruptly taking the bit and bolting.

Sheaves of raindrops beat against my face, my shoulders.

The surroundings grew darker and the headland and the villa were only dimly visible in the rain. The beach looked like an ink painting. I walked slowly along, still hoping for a glimpse of the little blonde girl. I knew she could not be out in this downpour. I knew that, but I still searched for her. What I wanted now was probably not the child herself, but rather the fantasy of seeing her. Of course, this was nonsense. I know that. But I believed then that I would not mind even just the fantasy.

The rain persisted. I carried on walking. I did not find the little blonde girl.

Little by little I grew tired, and the distinction between reality and illusion became hazy. I was losing my grip.

I was just seventeen, so why was reality so indistinct? Was it because I was still young? Or was it equally vague and unreliable for everybody? I would never find that little blonde girl I had seen yesterday playing with the crab, who had shouted fiercely, "*My* crab!" My blood had stained *her* breast a vivid red, but in the next moment it had become just one small dirty stain. Everything was hazy. Had I really beaten up a young man on the headland? I could no longer be confident of anything. The pain in my hand from having hit him had already gone. Plus I would never see those guys or their car on the headland again. There was no proof that the fight had ever happened, and I could no longer vouch that it had.

I was even beginning to think that dreams were more certain than reality. In my dream, I had shot her naked body. That dream would never change or fade. Every time I recalled it, her naked body would fall with bright red blood flowing from her white breast. That was certain.

It was still raining.

I was exhausted.

That night the wind raged. The TV and radio announced that the tropical storm off the coast of Kanto had strengthened and been upgraded to a typhoon.

Upstairs in my room, I pressed my face up to the window and stared out at the stormy night sea. Every now and then a heavy squall of rain spattered against the glass and passed by.

The sea was baring its white fangs. Its gentle face of indolence at the height of summer had gone. It had transformed. The sea tonight was violent and aggressive. This morning it betrayed me, defeated me. And now it was howling, as if challenging me.

Of a mind to accept the sea's challenge, I went out onto the balcony. I wanted to feel my body exposed to the wind and rain.

I was soon drenched to the skin. The rain was driving against me in large drops that hurt. The wind tried to sweep me off my feet. I braced myself, planting my feet firmly, and glared at the sea with my eyes wide open.

The wind and rain raged furiously, but then abruptly dropped. I continued to glare at the dark, boundlessly dark sea. In that blackness, I tried to recall everything that had happened to me since yesterday. I hoped that the roughness of the sea would expunge anything not worth remembering from my consciousness.

What on earth had I done these past two days? What had happened? I made an effort to remember. She was reading under the parasol. I swam. He arrived in his bright red sports car. I almost drowned. There was a young blonde girl. In my hands, a small crab was crushed to bits. I had fired the rifle at night on the headland, and I had touched her lips. And I had beaten up a young man. I could remember many things, but all the images were terribly vague. What had that little blonde girl's face looked like? I couldn't remember. Even the bright red drop of blood on *her* breast had dimmed. I was getting exasperated. Was reality as vague and nebulous for Yukibe as it was for me? No, it couldn't be. For her, there would surely always be a definite response to reality. That was probably why she had left school and home behind and taken to the streets. She had a clearly defined enemy to fight. But for me, it was as if there was a veil over my eyes and nothing at all was clear.

I wanted to shoot that veil away with the rifle. A momentary flash might make this vague, hazy reality into something unchanging and solid. It might clarify what I needed to do.

I went back into my room. I paid no attention to the water dripping from my drenched body as I took out my hunting rifle. Before loading it, I aimed it at the dark stormy sea. I would shoot at the sea, at the invisible veil. With my nerves on edge, my senses were keener than ever. That was probably why I noticed that something was not quite right. There was a slight difference in how it handled, and I noticed it right away. The gun was heavier than usual.

Did I leave it loaded?

No, that was not possible. I had no recollection of reloading it after firing it at the headland last night.

I checked the barrel. As I had thought, it wasn't loaded. But near the muzzle, I discovered something was blocking it; a ball of lead.

A chill ran down my spine. If, unawares, I had loaded the rifle and pulled the trigger, the weapon would have exploded and probably killed me.

Gradually the fear subsided. In its place, rage welled up. Who could have done such a thing?

It was him!

It must have been him. I could not think otherwise. It must have been him.

I had found a target for my bullet. The haze had not lifted from reality, but the enemy had become clear. This man was my enemy.

I took out my tools and removed the lump of lead; then I slowly loaded a bullet. My hands trembled slightly, not from fear but from the fury I felt towards him.

I took the gun and went downstairs.

The lights were off in the living room, but there was light coming from his room.

I threw open his door without knocking. He was sitting on the bed, and with a displeased expression looked at me and then at the gun.

"That's a dangerous thing you have there," he said.

I planted myself in the doorway and glared at him. His right hand was swathed in a white bandage. That whiteness reminded me of the incident that afternoon. I had hit him, and he had crashed into the window. The shattered glass. Dripping blood. Her eyes reproaching me. And her breast sullied by his blood.

"I'm going to kill you." I leveled the rifle at him. His face contorted in fear.

"Don't make dumb jokes," he said, his voice trembling. "What if it's loaded?"

"It is loaded. I am going to kill you."

"Why? Why would you do that?"

"Surely you know."

"No, I don't. I know you don't like me much, but is that enough for you to kill me?"

"You tried to kill me, so instead I'll kill you."

"I tried to kill you? What nonsense is that? I was your father's friend, you know. Why on earth would I want to kill you?"

"You blocked my gun with a lead ball so that it would explode and kill me. Isn't that so?"

"I put a lead ball in your gun? I don't know what you're talking about. I've never even touched your gun."

"You're lying."

"I'm not lying. You are like my own child. Your father himself asked me to look after you. And you think I would try to kill you?"

"So who put it there?"

"I don't know, but it wasn't me."

"You're the only one here. If it wasn't you—"

"What about her?" he said in a low voice. *Her?* I felt the blood drain from my face. A cold shiver ran through my body. It was not because I believed him. It was because she had suddenly come up in this dark talk about murder.

"It wasn't her," I yelled. "How could it be?"

"But if it wasn't me, that only leaves her," he said callously, his voice dry.

I shouted furiously, "No! It was you. You did it. And what about this morning? When you saw me drowning, you pretended you hadn't seen me and walked away. You intended to leave me for dead!"

"No. The fishing boat had seen you, so I knew you'd be alright. That's why I didn't do anything. Anyway, I can't swim."

"But why did you turn your back?"

"Ah, yes." His gaze went into space. "Yes, I did turn my back on you. That's because I noticed that she was on the upstairs balcony. I'm sure you won't believe me, but she was calmly watching you drown. Her face was so cold!"

"Liar!"

"It's true. At that moment, I again felt how you were a burden to her."

"It's a lie!"

"Do you remember me saying I wanted to give you some advice? I wanted to tell you to stop falling in love with her. You might think she's an angel, but she is the type of woman who cannot live without a man. She's been making eyes at me, too. So for her, you falling in love with her, being obsessed with her, is a nuisance. You're in her way."

"It's a lie! A lie!"

"It's cruel, but it's true. She was probably the one who fixed your gun."

"Rubbish! You haven't any proof."

"No, I don't have any proof. But there is a way of finding out if I am right or not. Go to her room and pretend that you are going to shoot her. If she is scared, then I am wrong. If she isn't scared, that's because she put the lead into the gun and knows that if you pull the trigger it'll be you who will die."

I was unsure what to do next. I just walked along the corridor to her room, and knocked on the door.

She opened the door.

I went in.

She was wearing a light, see-through negligée. It was as if she was standing naked before me.

"What's the matter?" She smiled gently at me, as if humoring a small child. Mechanically, I raised the rifle and silently aimed it at her breast.

"That's dangerous," she said. But her face showed no trace of fear. She did not even pale. That was not all. I saw a sinister glee in her eyes, as if she was expecting something. She knew. She knew, and was waiting for it—for the weapon to explode.

Strangely, I felt no anger. I merely felt confused. The worlds of reality and illusion had meshed within me, and I could not distinguish between them.

This is a dream.

This was the same as last night's dream.

If it was not a dream, surely I would not be able to shoot her. Therefore, it was a dream. It had to be a dream. In last night's dream, I shot her naked body with my hunting rifle. I could still clearly recall that dream. To my seventeen-year-old self, the dream was clearer than reality. If I did not pull the trigger now, it would become hazy like reality. Her image would transform into something elusive and vague. In order to make her mine I had to pull the trigger, just as I had in the dream.

Her naked body would fall slowly to the floor. Her breast would be stained with bright red blood. That vivid redness would remain unchanging for all eternity, because this was a dream.

I pulled the trigger.

The Monkey That Clapped Its Hands

Toku Yoshizawa's small body had remained motionless in the viewfinder for some time now. She squatted at the water's edge with her back hunched over, her hands coarsened by farm labor tightly clasped together, gazing out at the dull sheen of the sea. Seeing her silhouetted against the light, Sawaki could not make out her expression, but he guessed she was struggling to contain her tears.

He looked up from the camera at the officer from the local police station next to him.

The middle-aged policeman was clearly bored and itching to get back. It was only to be expected. As far as he was concerned, the case had been wrapped up a week ago—simply a young man's suicide, with nothing else suspicious about it. The fact that he did not come right out and say so was probably because he was more good-natured than his rough appearance suggested.

Sawaki took his cigarettes out of his pocket and offered one to the policeman. Shielding it with his body against the strong sea breeze he finally managed to light it, and then asked the officer, "Would you mind telling me about how the body was found?"

There was nothing much of any note in the policeman's story. A local fisherman had been taking his boat out that morning when he found the body washed up on the beach. That was all. The one point of interest for Sawaki was that the dead man had been clutching a small toy monkey in his hand when he drowned. That toy was now at the police station, along with his other personal effects.

Tossing his cigarette butt into the sea, the policeman turned to Sawaki with his head to one side. "I don't get it. Why would a reporter from Tokyo come all the way here to the Japan Sea for such an insignificant case?"

"Editor's orders," answered Sawaki simply. Indeed, for the police, this probably was a minor case of no importance. But there was someone who thought otherwise, and that was why Sawaki had come all the way from Tokyo, although he had no intention of telling the policeman that.

The dead youth's name was Shinkichi Yoshizawa. He was from a remote village in Hokkaido, and had come to Tokyo three years earlier having found employment at a laundry in Asakusa through the mass recruitment drive for school leavers from rural areas at that time. He was by all accounts a hard worker, and apparently sent part of his monthly wages back to his mother in Hokkaido. Yet, one day, this twenty-year-old man had suddenly gone off on a trip to the coast of Hokuriku and drowned himself.

What Sawaki had in mind was an investigative piece on the young man's life, to shed light on what might have driven him to suicide. In fact, he had not so much been ordered to do this by his editor as he had persuaded his editor to let him do it. It was partly his reaction against the newspaper's tendency to devote too many column inches to sensational stories like student protests and murders. He also hoped this "obscure" case might possibly illuminate the problematic nature of the mass recruitment program, but he did not yet know whether it would form part of this as a wider issue.

Sawaki once again turned his gaze back to Toku Yoshizawa.

The forty-seven-year-old mother bereaved of her only child was still sitting there gazing out to sea in exactly the same position as before.

Back at the police station, Sawaki took several photos of Toku collecting her son's belongings before picking out the toy monkey from among them.

It was the sort of toy often sold at night stalls for about five hundred yen. It held cymbals in each hand that it clapped together when you wound the screw. It was rusty from having been immersed in seawater, but as Sawaki wound it up there was an abrupt noisy clash of cymbals and the monkey started nodding its head jerkily back and forth. The sound was grotesquely amplified in the silent room, and he hurriedly stopped it with his hands.

"Was your son fond of toys like this?"

Toku briefly shook her dark, tanned face in answer to Sawaki's question. "He wasn't a child any more, and besides, he was always such a good boy, even when he was small."

At twenty years old, he was already an adult. And no doubt he was a dependable sort, just as she maintained. Yet he had been clutching this toy when he died. When Sawaki released his grip on it, the monkey clashed the cymbals together two or three times more before grinding to a halt.

"I just don't understand," said Toku, glancing distractedly at the toy monkey. "Why would he go and die, leaving me behind?"

"That's what I would like to know too," responded Sawaki.

Apart from the toy monkey, there was nothing of note among the dead man's belongings, but mixed in amongst the waterlogged pack of cigarettes and wallet containing less than five thousand yen, a book of matches bearing the name of a hotel caught Sawaki's eye. The Star Lily Inn. The policeman informed him that it was twelve or thirteen minutes' walk away.

"Let's go and check it out," Sawaki urged Toku, and together they left the police station.

The narrow road to the inn wound along the coast. The wind had picked up and the waves were tipped with white crests. There was nobody in sight, and no fishing boats on the water. To Sawaki, accustomed to the placid Shonan coastline near Tokyo, the early winter Hokuriku sea appeared dark and cheerless. Even if he wanted to die, he would not come here, he thought to himself. Why had young Shinkichi chosen this place to die?

Sawaki turned to Toku, who was lagging behind as usual. "Is this anything like the sea in Hokkaido?"

"What?" Toku glanced at him in surprise, before adding in a small voice, "No. In Utoro the sea is already icebound by now."

Sawaki had only ever been to Sapporo in Hokkaido, and he could not immediately place Utoro. If it was icebound, though, it must be further north, perhaps on the Sea of Okhotsk. Perhaps the sea where Toku and Shinkichi were from was even darker, even more desolate than here.

The Star Lily Inn was small, but solidly built in the old style with deep eaves to protect it against heavy snowfall. Sawaki blinked in the semi-darkness of the lobby.

The short, middle-aged desk clerk who came out to greet them immediately recalled Shinkichi Yoshizawa with a smile. "He's the one with a toy monkey, right?"

He must have been amused by a twenty-year-old man having a toy like that, thought Sawaki. Or perhaps he had found it ludicrous. Sawaki again wondered why Shinkichi had been carrying such a childish toy around with him as though it were a prized possession.

The clerk brought out the hotel register and showed it to them. Shinkichi Yoshizawa stayed there under his real name for one week. His handwriting was not elegant, but it had an earnest feel, almost excessively so. Toku's nose rubbed against the register as she peered at her son's handwriting, but after a while she raised her face and asked the clerk, "May I please see his room?"

The clerk called a maid to show Toku to the room. Sawaki would have liked to see it too, but he felt he should let Toku go alone and instead questioned the clerk about the last seven days of Shinkichi's life.

"As soon as he arrived, he wrote some letters," the clerk told him. Letters? Sawaki's eyes gleamed. If those had been suicide notes, they might learn the reason for his death.

"There were three altogether. At his request, I mailed them myself from the post office," added the clerk.

"Three letters?" It sounded even more likely to Sawaki that they were suicide notes, but it was strange that he had not sent one to his mother, Toku.

"I sent them express delivery. That's what he told me to do."

"Do you remember the contents of the letters?"

"Contents?" The clerk smiled wryly. "Well, they were in envelopes, you know."

"So how about the addressees? Can you at least remember whether they were sent to Hokkaido or Tokyo?"

"All three were to Tokyo."

That meant that none of them had been addressed to his mother.

"What about the names?" asked Sawaki.

The clerk rested his forehead on his hand as he considered this, but he could only recall one of them. His eyes shone as he told Sawaki, "It was the name of one of those experts that's always appearing on TV. He's pretty well known."

"An expert? You mean a college professor or social commentator, or something?"

"A commentator, that youngish guy who wears black-rimmed glasses. Name's Fuji-something-or-other."

"Fujishima? Kiichiro Fujishima?"

"Yes, that's the one. I'm sure of it."

Kiichiro Fujishima was an assistant professor at S University who had been making a name for himself as an up-and-coming commentator. Sawaki had met him once. He was extremely articulate and just the type of commentator popular on TV these days, although he was also criticized for being too much of a celebrity. In any case, he was famous. How come Shinkichi Yoshizawa had known him? Or could it be someone else of the same name? Sawaki could find out by paying Fujishima a visit upon his return to Tokyo.

"And after mailing the letters?" Sawaki pressed.

"He seemed to be waiting for something. Every day he would sit, looking out of the window and often asked about arrival times at the station and airport, and he was always checking to see if any mail had come for him," the clerk lowered his voice. It would appear that the three letters had not been intended as suicide notes, even if that was how they had ended up. Shinkichi Yoshizawa had spent a week at this inn waiting for the replies. When none came, he killed himself. What had Shinkichi written in those letters? Would he have still killed himself if he had received any replies? Why had the three recipients not replied or come up here to see him?

Toku had not returned. Sawaki suddenly felt uneasy and went upstairs to look for her. As he slid open the door of the tatami room with a sea view where Shinkichi had stayed, he was struck full in the face by the wind. Toku had flung the windows wide open and was sitting there gazing out to sea. Dusk was falling, and the breeze blowing in off the sea had an added chill to it. Frowning, Sawaki walked round to face her and said, "You'll catch cold."

Toku did not respond. She did not even appear to have heard him. She was not weeping, but she seemed abstracted, expressionless. Sawaki had no idea what she was thinking about.

That night Sawaki took Toku back to Tokyo on the overnight train. The journey took almost ten hours, during which time he snapped numerous photos of her. However, her expression in the viewfinder never changed and in the end he gave up and put the camera away. He would not be able to use photos like that. Instead, he tried asking her various things about her dead son, but the answers that came back were equally flat, certainly not the makings of a good story. The boy was well-behaved, a good kid. After his father died, he had left school as soon as he could, to go out to work. He had really looked after her. He had never quarreled with anyone else. After he came to Tokyo, he sent money home every month without fail. He had just written to her that he would soon be earning enough to bring her to live with him in Tokyo. So why did he go and kill himself? Why—

Why had he killed himself? Of course, Sawaki had no answer to that. He sat quietly trying to picture in his mind the twenty-year-old he had never met. The Shinkichi Yoshizawa he imagined from Toku's account was morally upright, thoroughly unfashionable, and utterly unnewsworthy. He sounded like a pretty dull kind of guy. Was it his deep earnestness that had driven him to suicide? Or had Toku over-idealized her only son, and in reality he had been a very different type of youth? Could he have changed after three years living in Tokyo?

They arrived at Ueno station early the next morning.

Tokyo was far warmer than Hokuriku, and as noisy and bustling as ever. They had breakfast in a café by the station, after which Sawaki told Toku he intended to pay Kiichiro Fujishima a visit. Toku, however, was reluctant to meet such an eminent figure. Sawaki was curious to see how Fujishima would respond to a farmer like her and tried to persuade her to go with him, but the more he tried to convince her, the more she recoiled from the idea.

There was no budging her, so for the time being he checked her into an inn by Shinobazu Pond, and went alone.

Kiichiro Fujishima lived in an upmarket condominium near Azabu Roppongi. It was certainly a sign of the times that such a young commentator could be living in a condo and drinking in the bars of Ginza. Sawaki called first to confirm he was home, and when he arrived, Fujishima came out to greet him with a big smile and showed him into the living room decorated with a floral-patterned carpet.

"You'd never believe how busy I am," he told Sawaki in a slight Kansai accent. "From next month I'll be serializing my opinion pieces, 'Youth Today: Reality and Myth' in your evening paper. That's going to take up a big chunk of my time."

"Thanks so much," Sawaki smiled. Fujishima complained of being busy, but he looked healthy and full of energy, and appeared to be rather enjoying the frenzy of activity. A pretty young girl he introduced as his secretary brought them coffee. Sawaki felt a twinge of envy for this commentator who seemed to be surrounded by a swirl of brilliant color.

Fujishima lit up a slim cigar and then looked at Sawaki. "So, what brings you here today?" The mild scent of the cigar tickled Sawaki's nose. He had been offered one, but instead took out his own pack of Hi-Lites.

"The matter of a young man's suicide."

"Ah, the youth suicide issue," nodded Fujishima. "A huge problem, particularly in this country. First of all—"

In characteristically eloquent fashion, he rattled off how the youth suicide rate in Japan was the highest in the civilized world, how many youngsters had killed themselves in the past year and for what reasons, as well what measures against youth suicide were being taken in different countries. It was as though there were a number of drawers in his head, and whenever a specific issue cropped up the corresponding drawer automatically opened and the answers came flying out. Being able to instantly come up with answers for all manner of social issues was a valued talent in today's media, but for Sawaki, who had come to talk about one particular young man's death, Fujishima's intelligent, perfectly calibrated talk felt strangely lacking. Once he had made his main points, Sawaki quickly grasped the opportunity to interrupt.

"The young man in question was apparently an acquaintance of yours."

"Is that so? In that case, he must have been a student at my university. If I'm perfectly frank with you, the university has now become so absolutely ginormous that unless he stood out for any reason I would never remember him. Not to mention the upheaval of the campus protests, ha ha ha!" he said, laughing off any sense of responsibility.

"No, he can't have been your student."

"In which case, I'm even more in the dark."

"His name was Shinkichi Yoshizawa. A twenty-year-old."

"Yoshizawa?" Fujishima furrowed his brows. He appeared to have no memory of him.

"A week before he died, I believe he sent you a letter," added Sawaki.

Fujishima called his secretary. "Miss Miyoshi, look and see if a letter came from someone called Shinkichi Yoshizawa, would you?"

The secretary nodded wordlessly and disappeared into the office, returning immediately with a sealed letter. Pinned to the envelope was a typewritten page. While Fujishima was casting his eyes over the page, the young woman took a seat next to him and, crossing her shapely legs, opened up a notepad on her knee. Sawaki thought he had seen this somewhere before, and then realized it was a scene from an American movie. It was the classic pairing of a dynamic executive and his beautiful and capable secretary. Sawaki smiled wryly.

"Now I get it," said Fujishima. "Yes, the letter did arrive. This appears to be it."

Sawaki glanced at the envelope Fujishima passed him. The sender was indeed Shinkichi Yoshizawa. The handwriting was the same as in the register at the Star Lily Inn.

"I have a number of top-class brains working under me," Fujishima said running his eyes over the attached sheet of paper. "Most are graduate students, and according to this memorandum,

Utsumi was in charge of this case. He has been away in England, so the reply was pending his return."

Sawaki did not quite understand what Fujishima meant by being in charge of the case, but he wanted to read the letter, so with Fujishima's permission he opened the envelope.

Dear Dr. Kiichiro Fujishima,

My name is Shinkichi Yoshizawa. I have never met you, but I wrote to you about a year ago. I did not expect to hear back from someone as famous as yourself, so when I received your conscientious reply it was like a dream come true. I cannot tell you how much that letter encouraged me. I tend to get very lonely, and just the fact that a famous professor like you could be concerned about a nobody like me, gave me the support I needed.

But now I again feel that life is unbearable. I guess I'm not as strong as you said.

I am staying at a small hotel in Hokuriku called the Star Lily Inn. I plan to be here for one week. I know it is selfish of me to ask this of you, but I would really like to receive another encouraging letter from you while I am here. I am sure that if you write to me, I will again find the courage I need.

I look forward to hearing from you.

There was nothing in the letter to suggest Shinkichi had been contemplating suicide, and the contents were pretty vague. What was clear, though, was that he wanted a reply. He had been waiting in that musty old inn in Hokuriku just to hear from Kiichiro Fujishima. And that reply was never sent.

"It was one of your brains, Tetsuo Utsumi, who replied last year," said the secretary in her clear alto voice.

"I share out responsibilities amongst my students," said Fujishima by way of explanation. "Whenever we receive a letter, whoever replies to it assumes responsibility for any subsequent correspondence. Other less concerned commentators would not even consider replying, but I just can't bring myself not to.

So I have a team of around twenty brains working on it. Of course I pay them out of my own pocket, and I'm always reminding them about their duty. In this case, too, Miss Miyoshi no doubt thought it appropriate for Utsumi to reply, and was keeping it until he got back from his trip."

Sawaki remained silent, watching Fujishima's mouth moving. Fujishima looked quite self-satisfied, but for all he bandied words like "person in charge," "brains," "responsibility," and so forth, in the end, all it amounted to was getting his students to ghostwrite his replies for him, wasn't it? But there was hardly any point in saying so. Ghostwriting in that world was par for the course, and if anything Fujishima's way of doing things was, as he said, conscientious. After all, he had sent a reply to a total stranger, even if it had been ghostwritten.

Nevertheless, if he had not been so concerned about getting the same person to write the second time, Shinkichi Yoshizawa would probably still be alive today.

This bothered Sawaki. To put it even more bluntly, if no reply had been sent the first time, perhaps Shinkichi would not have set so much store by Fujishima. However Sawaki did not voice this either. To some extent, ghostwriting itself entailed relinquishing responsibility, so there was absolutely no point grilling Fujishima over his responsibility for a young man's death. Plus Sawaki also felt that it was not he who should get angry with Fujishima, but Toku Yoshizawa.

When Sawaki requested permission to keep the letter, Fujishima readily answered, "By all means."

Sawaki asked just one last question.

"What would you think of a twenty-year-old guy with a wind-up toy monkey as a prized possession?"

"Sounds like a bit of a loser to me," grinned Fujishima. "It suggests feminization. A guy like that doesn't belong in today's world. Men of his age should be grappling with something bigger than that."

So he killed himself.

Sawaki kept the thought to himself.

Back at the inn, Sawaki had expected Toku to react angrily when he gave her the letter addressed to Kiichiro Fujishima. At least that was what he was secretly hoping. He switched on his tape recorder at the ready.

Yet Toku said nothing even after reading her son's letter. He had kept the tape running in vain. Sawaki grew more and more irritated. He had in mind a particular scenario in which a mother who had lost her only son vented her anger against a social commentator turned celebrity who had acted irresponsibly. However clichéd it might sound, if it served to highlight the young man's death then he would be able to make an article out of it, but it all hung on Toku. If she maintained her silence, then nothing would come of it.

"If your son had received a reply to that letter, he might not have committed suicide. Don't you agree?" he said, half trying to goad a reaction out of her. The suggestion of a tremor briefly ran across Toku's features, but the words that eventually came out of her mouth were not those Sawaki was hoping to hear.

"But such a famous professor must be terribly busy—"

"But hey, that doesn't mean he isn't responsible. After all, someone died."

Toku looked flustered by Sawaki's raised voice. "Thank you very much," she said, abruptly bowing her head. "I had completely forgotten to thank you."

"That's not what I meant!" grimaced Sawaki. It looked as though it would be impossible to get Toku to denounce Kiichiro Fujishima.

"There must be two more letters from your son. Shall we go looking for them?" he said, changing the subject.

They went out after lunch.

Sawaki just did not understand Toku. He understood her grief at losing her only son, but surely she was angry too? Perhaps she was still too immersed in her sorrow. Or maybe she was overwhelmed by Tokyo, this being her first visit to the capital.

First Sawaki took her to the laundry in Asakusa where Shinkichi had worked. It was quite a large shop, with three brand-new automatic washing machines lined up at the front of the store. When Sawaki stated the reason for their visit, the plump proprietor showed them into the living room at the back.

"He was such a good boy. I still can't believe he killed himself," said the kindly looking man, looking alternately at Sawaki and Toku. Shinkichi had been a hardworking boy, and he had even raised his salary and could not think of any reason why he might have killed himself. The proprietor did not give the impression he was saying such things to be kind to Toku. He certainly did seem to find it an inconvenience that he was understaffed, having lost such a good worker.

"Did you receive a letter from him after he went away?"

"Yes, one did come," the proprietor assented. "But it wasn't addressed to me. It was to Miyamoto, the lad who worked with him."

"Can we talk to him?"

"He's already left. Straight after Yoshizawa went away, it was."

"So what about the letter?"

"I sent it on to him."

"So where is this Miyamoto now?"

"Last I heard he was working at that cabaret up the road. Chat Noir, it's called. The nightlife business is all that type of lad is good for, they think it's easy money," he smiled sardonically at Sawaki.

Sawaki turned to Toku. "Shall we go and take a look?" She seemed a bit taken aback by the idea of going to a cabaret, but agreed to go.

They saw the Chat Noir as soon as they went out onto the main street, Kokusai Dori. Its enormous neon sign featuring a black cat was just beginning to flicker into life. However, Miyamoto had already left and they were told he was now working in a bar called Violet in Ikebukuro. Sawaki was shocked at such a drastic move, but he and Toku immediately hailed a taxi to take them to Ikebukuro.

They found Miyamoto working there as a bartender. Sawaki had imagined him to be a yakuza type, but he turned out to be a cheerful fresh-faced young man of about twenty-one or twenty-two.

"Anyone who hangs around wasting their time as a server in a cabaret is an idiot," laughed Miyamoto proudly. Sawaki was unfamiliar with this world and had no idea whether a server or a bartender was the higher rank, but looking at the youth's self-satisfied air, he guessed the bartender was the more important. When he introduced Toku Yoshizawa, Miyamoto said, "Oh, so

you're Shinkichi's mother?" as he deftly took an orange juice from
the refrigerator.

Sawaki was half impressed by his smooth manner, but he also
felt something rather cold about it. The youth seemed even more
worldly wise than Sawaki was at thirty-two, although Sawaki did
not feel much sincerity in him. But that was probably what was
considered "cool."

After taking a sip from the highball placed in front of him by
Miyamoto, Sawaki ventured, "I believe Yoshizawa sent you a letter
before he died?"

"Yeah," agreed Miyamoto.

"Have you got that letter with you now?"

"I guess. Wait here a moment, please."

Miyamoto whispered something to the manageress before
leaving the bar and going upstairs.

Toku sat stiffly leaving her juice untouched. She was apparently
ill at ease in the bar. Sawaki had just said a few words to her in an
effort to put her at ease when Miyamoto returned with the letter.

I'm in a small inn in Hokuriku right now. It's called the Star
Lily Inn. I told everyone at work that I wanted to go on a
trip, but the truth is I ran away. I don't really understand it
myself, but I've somehow lost my confidence at work, and
I'm feeling so scared I can't bear it. You'll probably laugh,
but living in Tokyo is really scary. I envy you. You're brave.
Probably only people like you are capable of living in Tokyo.

You said that working in the laundry was really dumb and
that you were going to work in a nightclub or something,
but I don't think I can do that. But then, I don't want stay
in the same job—that scares me, too. I can't really explain,
but I feel like I've been shut up inside a small box and I can't
breathe. Won't you come up here now? If I go back to Tokyo
in this state, I get the feeling I'll be stuck in the same rut again.
I want to be able to talk to you here, whilst looking out to sea.
I think, if I can do that, I'll be able to get the courage I need.

Please come. There should be two thousand yen in my
desk drawer, so use it to pay for the travel expenses.

There was nothing that hinted of death in this letter either. Compared to the one sent to Kiichiro Fujishima there was a heightened sense of anxiety, but even so the contents were pretty vague, and as for the part about feeling like he was in a small box— Sawaki could not quite fathom the precise nature of his unease.

"So in the end you didn't go, right?"

Miyamoto shrugged, and fiddled with the lighter in his hand. "What could I do? I'd just started at the bar, so no way could I take time off already. The first weeks are crucial, see? And anyway, I never thought he'd go and kill himself. He never said anything about suicide."

"He says here that he was scared to go on living."

"Isn't everyone? Life in Tokyo is tough."

There was something flippant about the way he said this. Perhaps it was "cool" for youngsters to make light of serious issues. Sawaki did not know whether to put it down to youthful self-consciousness or to pluck. All he did know was that Shinkichi Yoshizawa did not have the ability to make fun of life.

"Why do you think he killed himself?"

"How should I know?" retorted Miyamoto rolling his eyes up at the ceiling. "I can't be expected to know what someone else was feeling."

"What sort of person would you say Yoshizawa was?"

"A good guy. Strong, but kind. Although you could say that was his problem. These days, the bad guys tend to win out."

These days, huh?

Sawaki smiled sourly. What sort of worldview did this youngster have? And what about poor Yoshizawa?

"But it's a bummer he died," muttered Miyamoto under his breath, then turned to Toku and smiled. "Would you prefer some Coke?" There wasn't even a trace of a shadow behind his smile. He appeared absolutely unaffected by the death of his friend. Sawaki realized that any further questioning would be fruitless, but he wanted to find out who the third letter had been written to. When he asked Miyamoto whether he had any idea at all who it could be, the youth thought for a moment.

"It must have been her."

"Her?"

"Akiko Shimojo. There's a bakery near the laundry in Asakusa. She's the daughter of the people who run it. She's quite cute, and he seemed to have a thing for her."

Sawaki asked for the name of the shop and was on his way out with Toku when Miyamoto turned to her and said smoothly, "One of these days, with your permission, I would like to visit Shinkichi's grave." He was hardly sincere in the way he said it, yet Toku politely bowed her head and said, "Thank you."

Unfortunately a "Closed" sign hung in the window of Shimojo Confectioners in the Senzoku district of Asakusa. Sawaki tried ringing the bell just in case, but there was no answer. Reluctantly he decided to try again the following day. He put Toku in a taxi back to the inn in Ueno and then dropped by the newspaper office.

After listening to Sawaki's account, the desk editor, as might have been predicted, grimaced. "Not much to go on, is there?" he commented. "It all hangs on why he committed suicide. Look, I let you go for it because you said it wouldn't be just a broken heart or money problems or anything like that. You said it was a social issue affecting all the kids brought into the city from the provinces on the recruitment program. But now you're telling me you haven't dug up anything specific, and not even the mother's angry about losing her only son. Doesn't sound like you've got much of a story!"

"I know, I know," said Sawaki resignedly. He was far from satisfied himself. He had managed to find two of the letters, but however many times he read them, he could not find any motive for suicide in them. And then there was Toku's attitude. Why wasn't she angry?

"How about turning up the heat on her a bit?" asked the desk editor, tapping the end of his pencil on the desk. "Tomorrow you're going to meet the recipient of the last letter, right?"

"Assuming the third letter was addressed to Akiko Shimojo."

"Right. If she had replied, then surely Yoshizawa wouldn't have killed himself. His mother must be feeling angry and resentful that she didn't bother. You've got to provoke her into showing that. Get Toku to slap that girl's face. If you get a photo like that, I'll be able to use it. I'll caption it 'Rage of a mother robbed of her son'."

"But that doesn't help us know what it was that robbed a young man of his life, you know."

"So find out. Quickly."

"Yeah, alright." Sawaki shrugged, and then produced the toy monkey he had borrowed off Toku. "I don't know why, but Yoshizawa was clutching this when he died."

"A cheap toy like this?" The desk editor turned it over in his stubby fingers examining it, then wound it up. The toy monkey started crashing the cymbals together, but it sounded far feebler than it had in Hokuriku, perhaps because of the surrounding hubbub of the city news office.

"Simple," said the desk editor absentmindedly. Sawaki stared at him blankly. "This toy," he jutted his chin at it, "must have been a present from some girl he liked. That's why it was so important to him. He probably got it from that Akiko Shimojo."

It was clear that the desk editor had formed a specific image of Shinkichi Yoshizawa as a virtuous but timid and sentimental young man. Sawaki recalled what Kiichiro Fujishima had said about it being symbolic of Yoshizawa's feminization. For all the commentator's high-blown language, his image of Yoshizawa was probably not so very different to the desk editor's now.

Sawaki was not so sure. This was partly due to his cautious nature, but it also had to do with being directly involved in the investigation. Having seen with his own eyes the dark sea in Hokuriku where the young man had chosen to die, and having spent two days with Toku, he was reluctant to make any hasty judgments.

Sawaki gazed doubtfully at the toy monkey, now still. Was it really as the desk editor claimed, that Yoshizawa had treasured it up until the moment he died because he had been given it by some girl he liked? Was that all it was?

The next day, Sawaki took a company car and went to pick up Toku from the inn in Ueno. When he asked the maid how Toku had been. She said she had spent all the time shut up in her room and had not taken even a single step outside. Unaware of the circumstances, the dissatisfied maid complained, "I suggested she visit Sensoji temple in Asakusa, but she didn't even do that."

Sawaki tried to imagine how Toku must have looked, but all he could see was that stiff, hard expression of hers. What Sawaki wanted to know was what lay beyond that stony face, but he was not at all confident he would discover it today, either.

When Toku came downstairs, she bowed deeply to Sawaki and said, "I'm sorry for all the trouble I'm causing you."

Her face showed signs of exhaustion, and her eyes were red-rimmed and bloodshot. She probably had not slept well last night, thought Sawaki, but he deliberately did not express any sympathy as he took her out to the car. If Toku's nerves were on edge, there was more likelihood of getting her to slap the girl's face as the desk editor was hoping. He was also concerned that by hiding her feelings and putting her defenses up, any misplaced sympathy would result in those defenses becoming even more impenetrable. Today he felt it better to keep an eye on Toku from a distance. That way he might get to see her true feelings.

Today Shimojo Confectioners was open. It was almost noon by the time they arrived there, and the shop was crowded with local office workers, male and female.

Sawaki waited for the shop to clear before taking Toku in. He handed his business card to the middle-aged woman behind the counter, and asked after Akiko. The woman looked at Sawaki, and then again at his business card before replying, "My daughter is not back from work yet."

Her expression revealed curiosity tinged with wariness, no doubt because of the newspaper's name printed on the business card. When he asked whether he could meet Akiko, the woman replied that she would be home after six o'clock.

"She started at M Trading a couple of weeks ago. That's in Marunouchi—" She seemed proud that her daughter was employed at a well-known company. The way she had emphasized Marunouchi, the upmarket business district around Tokyo Station, gave her a rather old-fashioned air.

Sawaki introduced Toku to her. The woman did not appear to recognize Shinkichi Yoshizawa's name at first, but when Sawaki mentioned the name of the laundry she at last went "Ah! Is he the one who committed suicide recently?"

"That's right," assented Sawaki, his heart sinking. From her reaction, it did not appear that the relationship between Akiko and Shinkichi had been all that strong. Even if Akiko had been the recipient of the third letter, they would probably be none the wiser about the reason for his suicide.

Sawaki and Toku left the shop intending to return soon after six o'clock. In the intervening hours, Sawaki showed Toku around Asakusa's Sensoji temple and Space Tower. However, Toku never once relaxed her rigid expression. She followed Sawaki around in silence, showing no irritation or any other emotion even when he turned his camera on her.

When they returned to the bakery, Akiko Shimojo was back from work. Just as Miyamoto had said, she was cute, with a round face, and about eighteen or nineteen years of age.

"I heard you work at M Trading," ventured Sawaki.

"It was so boring working in the bakery!" said Akiko innocently. "Working here I'd never meet anyone worth mentioning. The customers here are all liquor shop boys or sushi chefs. You get some office workers too, but they're all from small companies. A bunch of losers. That's why I joined M Trading. All the guys there went to university and have a future."

Listening to her, Sawaki felt his mouth widening into a sardonic smile. Having worked in a laundry, Shinkichi Yoshizawa was exactly the sort of loser that Akiko would think not worth mentioning. Sawaki had introduced Toku as Shinkichi's mother, but that did not stop Akiko from saying such things to her face. He could not help smiling at her pluck. Perhaps such artlessness was considered "cool" these days.

"Did Shinkichi happen to send you a letter?"

"Letter?" repeated Akiko blankly. "Yeah, maybe," she added vaguely. Jumping to her feet, she said she would go and look for it and disappeared inside. It was nearly ten minutes before she came back. "Here it is," she said, handing over an unopened letter.

"Didn't you read it?" Sawaki asked.

"No."

"Why not?"

"Because it's nothing to do with me."

"What do you mean, nothing to do with you?"

"I mean I'm not interested. And besides, I'm dating someone else."

"So he wasn't your boyfriend, then?"

"Boyfriend?" snickered Akiko. "He wasn't my type. He was a serious sort, but there's not much of a future working in a laundry, is there?"

She was not in the slightest bothered about how she said it. It seemed that "a future" was her mantra. In Akiko's mind, the opposite sex was apparently divided simply into two types: men with a future and men without. It seemed Shinkichi Yoshizawa had unfortunately been classified as the latter. And Akiko's new boyfriend was no doubt an elite employee of M Trading, a university graduate with a promising future. Sawaki was more amused than angry.

Wordlessly, Sawaki opened the envelope.

I'm in Hokuriku. The boss gave me some days off so I came here. Apparently he gave me special leave because I work so hard. At this rate, he said, in five or six years he'll be able to let me run the store. If I become a store manager, I'll earn easily 100,000 yen, I reckon. Of course, I won't be satisfied with just managing one small store. In the future, I plan to have my own store, make it into a company, and have a chain of stores all over Tokyo.

The reason I'm writing this to you Aki is that I want you to know what sort of guy I am. I want you to know that I'm not the sort of guy to be satisfied with working as an assistant in a laundry. People should dream big, right? Miyamoto told me you like sports cars, and I'm sure that one of these days I'll be able to buy one. I've already got my driver's license.

Aki, you really look like that actress, N—Miyamoto thinks she's childish and he doesn't like her, but I do. I think she's pure.

I'm going to stay here for a week. I'd really like for you to write me back while I'm here, Aki. Please tell me what you think of me. I find it difficult to say what I want whenever I meet you in Tokyo, so please write to me while I'm here.

Sawaki was dumbfounded. He had expected this of all the letters to be full of reproach, but if he had hoped to learn the reason for the suicide from it he was disappointed.

This letter did not reveal even a trace of the vague anxiety that permeated the other two. It reminded Sawaki of a rooster shaking its crest at a hen, flaunting itself to get attention. It was absolutely not the sort of letter you would expect from a young man about to commit suicide. Sawaki stared at Akiko, baffled. No two ways about it, this was a love letter.

"What does it say?" asked Akiko.

"That he's in love with you," Sawaki answered, and she grinned.

"Then I should have read it after all."

"Why's that?"

"Because it's fun!"

"But he killed himself."

"Because of me?"

"If that was the case, what would you think?"

"Hmm. Kind of flattered, kind of sad..." answered Akiko in a singsong voice.

The more Sawaki talked to her, the more he felt irritated. He felt like he was discussing the plot of a romantic movie, not a young man who had just committed suicide.

Changing the subject, he asked her about the toy monkey.

"No idea," she said flatly. "I never gave him anything."

"Really?"

"Really. He meant nothing to me, so why would I give him a present? Weird."

Sawaki was lost for words. It seemed the desk editor had got it completely wrong. Sawaki should have felt vindicated, but instead he just felt even more baffled.

He had forgotten all about the desk editor's instructions to goad Toku into slapping Akiko's face. He felt utterly wrong-footed by the contents of the letter being so different to what he had imagined. Far from gaining any insight into Shinkichi Yoshizawa's suicide, he felt even further from the truth. He was no closer to goading Toku into anything. After reading the letter, Toku herself merely asked Akiko, "Would you be so kind as to let me have this letter?"

Toku wanted to return to Hokkaido right away, but Sawaki pressured her into staying one more day. For what it was worth, he reported the encounter with Akiko Shimojo back to the desk editor. At this rate, it did not look as though he would ever get a story.

After hearing Sawaki out, the desk editor put an unexpectedly bright face on things. "Come on, cheer up!"

Sawaki said glumly, "I just don't understand young people today." It was the truth. He had considered himself young, but now he felt a chasm had opened up between him and the younger generation. He had no better understanding of the young bartender Miyamoto than he did Akiko Shimojo. More than anything, he had no idea what had been going on in Shinkichi Yoshizawa's head. How could anyone write such a naively optimistic love letter just before killing himself?

"Oh, I understand them alright," laughed the desk editor. "Not that I sympathize with them, mind you. It's just that their way of thinking is simple."

"But how are we supposed to interpret that last letter? It was obviously a love letter, and a wildly optimistic one at that—"

"That's easy. You're trying to read too much into it. Youngsters these days don't think that deeply about things. Shinkichi Yoshizawa is simply trying to show his best side to a girl he likes. That's all. Like you said, it's a rooster shaking its crest at a hen."

"I know that. What I don't understand is why someone about to commit suicide would send off such a sweet letter. It's so different from the other two letters, don't you think? First of all—"

"No, I don't think so," interrupted the desk editor with a frown. "They might look different at first glance, but they do have one thing in common."

"What's that?"

"The fact that he wanted an answer from them. In all the letters, he asked them to reply, or even come to Hokuriku, within the week."

"That's true, but—"

"I think what Shinkichi Yoshizawa wanted to convey in the letter was probably just that: please reply, please join me. That's all. Everything else was just a way to get the addressee's attention. So for Kiichiro Fujishima he starts off by thanking him effusively for the previous response, and he tells his mate Miyamoto that he is so brave—"

"And Akiko Shimojo that she looks like that actress."

"Exactly."

"But why was he so desperate for a reply? Would getting a reply have stopped him from killing himself?"

"This is only conjecture, but I reckon that Shinkichi Yoshizawa made a bet with himself."

"A bet…?"

"Uh-huh. There's nothing to suggest suicide in the letters. But he does sound lonesome. It is sometimes said that the worst thing for all the kids brought in from the provinces to work in Tokyo is the sense of isolation. Shinkichi Yoshizawa must also have felt that he was all alone here. And what he must have wanted more than anything else was assurance that he wasn't alone—so to get that assurance, he wrote to the three people he trusted most. In other words, he made a bet."

"So you're saying he lost the bet?"

"Yup. He probably thought that if he received just one reply he would try to make a go of things again."

"That's an interesting idea, but…"

"But what?"

"If that's the case, why didn't say he was going to kill himself? If he had written that he would kill himself unless he received an answer, the chances of getting a reply would have been higher, wouldn't they?"

"You're forgetting about self-respect," chuckled the desk editor. "A twenty-year-old has a strong sense of pride. That would have been going too far—and getting a reply after threatening them with suicide would hardly count as winning a bet now, would it."

The desk editor seemed pretty confident of his opinion. Sawaki thought that there might indeed be something in it—and if so, then it followed that had just one person replied or gone to Hokuriku, Shinkichi Yoshizawa would be alive today. If they ran an article with the headline "Youth wagered life on three letters," they would effectively be denouncing Kiichiro Fujishima, Miyamoto, and Akiko Shimojo. Indeed, thought Sawaki, all three certainly bore some of the responsibility for Shinkichi Yoshizawa's death although none of them appeared to realize it.

But there were still too many unanswered questions. What was the significance of the toy monkey? What feelings was Toku concealing behind her stony expression?

"I still don't understand why he killed himself," shrugged Sawaki.

"Perhaps he just couldn't handle the tough life in the city," suggested the desk editor.

"But he's from Utoro!"

"Utoro?"

"It's on the north-eastern tip of Hokkaido. I've never been there, but looking on the map it's midway up the Shiretoko Peninsula. It's a fishing village on the Sea of Okhotsk, and is hemmed in by ice floes during the winter. It hasn't even got a railway!"

"You're preaching to me about the geography of Hokkaido?"

"What I'm trying to say is that Shinkichi Yoshizawa was born and raised in a harsh natural environment. Life in Tokyo can't be that tough, can it? I just don't get it."

"If that's how you feel, then why don't you accompany Toku Yoshizawa when she goes home?"

"I would like to," said Sawaki vaguely. "But unless she loosens up, I still won't have a story. Also, I can't help thinking the reason for Shinkichi's suicide has got to be in Tokyo..." he concluded doubtfully.

"I guess you're right," said the desk editor, nonchalantly countering his own proposal. He probably had not intended it to be taken seriously in the first place.

The next day, still feeling ambivalent, Sawaki saw Toku off at Ueno Station. Her expression was as hard as ever. As they waited for the train to depart, Sawaki showered her with questions in an attempt to elicit something that he could use for an article, but all he could get out of her was a repeated, "Thank you for all you've done." At this rate he had nothing to gain by going back to Hokkaido with her, he thought.

Just as the train was about to depart, he casually said, "Do come back to Tokyo sometime!"

He had expected a simple "Thank you" by way of answer, but Toku said forcefully, "No, I won't," and shook her head. "I never want to set foot here ever again!"

Sawaki felt as though he had been slapped across the face. It was the first time Toku had ever shown any anger, and it was directed at Tokyo, the city that had caused the death of her only son.

"Mrs. Yoshizawa," he said hastily, but the train started moving and Toku slammed the window shut. She did not look back.

Sawaki stared in astonishment as the train departed. Coming to his senses, he raced to the nearest public telephone, grabbed the receiver and dialed the number for the newspaper.

"Is that the desk editor? I'm getting the next train for Hokkaido."

Sawaki had often felt he would like to see the ice floes of the Sea of Okhotsk. Now that very scene was there before his eyes. A huge white mass blanketed the port and the coast, and the brief patches of seawater appeared strangely black. Locked in ice, the sea looked as if it had given up any pretence of functioning as a sea and was plunged in a deep sleep.

It was not just the sea that was asleep. The land, too, was under deep snow and the villages appeared immersed in slumber. There was no sign of people.

Due to the snow, the train arrived several hours late in Shari. The last bus to Utoro had long since departed, and so Sawaki had to make do with a horse-drawn sled.

The strong wind along the coastal road prevented the powdery snow from accumulating, making the road icy. It was freezing. The Hokuriku coast had been cold too, but this was on another level altogether. The wind on Sawaki's face was so cold it hurt. He concentrated all his energy on huddling up his body on the sled and keeping his face hidden. He doubted he would survive even a single day in such a place. Nature here was too cruel. Shivering on the sled, he again felt the same doubt welling up. Why would anyone raised in such a harsh natural environment be defeated by life in Tokyo?

Utoro was an impoverished fishing village, a row of humble shack-like dwellings clinging to the shore. Toku Yoshizawa's house was one of these.

By the time Sawaki got off the sled, his body was frozen through. The wind blowing in from the sea sent the snow whirling up, while the Shiretoko mountain range loomed behind.

This is not a place for human habitation.

Here there were just mountains and sea, thought Sawaki. And the sea is dead, closed in by ice. The sense of isolation would probably drive him out of his mind.

Toku greeted Sawaki with a look of surprise and took him to sit by the sunken hearth. Sipping the hot tea she made him, he at last began to feel himself again.

Adding some more wood to the fire, Toku said, "I was just about to burn those letters." The stony expression she had worn in Tokyo was gone without trace.

"You're not going to put them in Shinkichi's grave?" asked Sawaki, warming his hands over the flames.

Toku smiled. "That's what I thought at first, but then I worried he might feel humiliated even in death. That wouldn't do."

"I see what you mean," agreed Sawaki. Indeed, those three letters that had remained unanswered could only be hurtful for the dead youth.

Toku threw the three letters into the flames, one by one. Within seconds they were burned to cinders. Sawaki felt a pang in his chest at the sheer speed at which they had disappeared.

Toku sat for a while in silence stirring the ash with the tongs, then got up and went into the other room, coming back with an old wooden apple crate. Inside were Shinkichi's diary and books, which she also planned to burn. When he heard the word "diary," Sawaki asked if he might take a look.

The diary consisted of three close-ruled school notebooks. They were not a continuous record, but rather a series of random jottings with much blank space between. While Sawaki ran his eyes over the pages, Toku ripped up the magazines and books and fed them little by little into the flames. In the intermittent flares of light, Sawaki continued reading.

He did not come across any passages that particularly stood out. Most of it was conventional, and tedious to read. There were the usual pretentious comments typical of teenagers.

In the third notebook there was a poem. No, he was not sure you could call it a poem. It was too clumsy, too full of youthful angst.

I like it here
Summer is short and winter long
Harvests are lean and nature harsh
But I like it here
Why?
Because here nature calls to me
Like in a fairytale world
The murmuring treetops startle me,
The fish from the sea
Play hide-and-seek in the rock pools
And when the snow piles up higher than the roofs
I make a snowman and it beams at me
Then in summer
When I fall asleep on the beach
All the clouds in the sky
All the fishes and birds
Even the wind from the north
All together they envelop me
With their noisy chatter
And so
I like it here

Sawaki skimmed through it not paying much attention, but then something struck him and he hastily turned the page back. Reading it another two or three times, he got the feeling that there was something extraordinarily meaningful in this poem.

Nature in Utoro was cruel. Yet according to this poem, Shinkichi Yoshizawa had not felt lonely here. Here nature was always talking to him, but perhaps in Tokyo the artificial environment had not spoken to him at all?

Could it be that Shinkichi had been consumed by loneliness even while surrounded by people? The city that never spoke to him, as he wrote in his letter to Miyamoto, must have been as claustrophobic as being shut up in a small box. Without nature to talk to him, the only means of escaping the loneliness was to find a mentor, friend, or lover with whom he could converse. That was why he had written those three letters. But just like Tokyo's artificial environment, they too failed to answer him. That was why...

Sawaki went outside the house without making a sound.

The wind was still raging. Embarrassed at the childishness of what he was doing, he tried listening to the wind. But try as he might, all he could hear was a bleak howl. His hands numb with cold, he made a little snowman. But the snowman was nothing more than a lump of snow and did not talk to him or even smile at him.

There's no reason why I should be able to hear nature's voice.

Sawaki shrugged. His ears were attuned to the noise of the city, so why would he be able to hear nature's voice? Even if nature did talk to him, he had lost the ability to understand it.

Shinkichi Yoshizawa had spent three years in Tokyo, hadn't he?

The thought suddenly occurred to him. He gazed out over the icebound Sea of Okhotsk as if seeking answers there.

The fact that Shinkichi had not received any replies to the three letters he sent, hoping to alleviate the unbearable loneliness of the city was probably not the only reason he had had committed suicide. Gazing out to sea in Hokuriku, perhaps he realized that he could no longer hear nature's voice. Such a realization must have exacerbated his despair, and perhaps he had lost even the courage to return home. Or maybe it was just Sawaki's imagination working overtime. Perhaps he was getting overly sentimental.

Sawaki went back inside the house to find Toku still burning books and magazines. As he took a seat by the hearth, he asked, "Will you burn this diary too?"

Toku replied that that was her intention. After slowly lighting up a cigarette, Sawaki told her, "You should put it in his grave with him. He needs some company, after all."

Toku looked at him in silence, then smiled and assented, "Okay, let's do that."

Sawaki felt relieved. That poem at least should be buried together with him. He knew he was being terribly sentimental. That was a word he detested, but right now he thought that once in a while it was even good to get sentimental without beating yourself up about it. It was a bit like reminiscing on childhood. While he had been outside making the snowman, Sawaki had recalled being a child. Had nature talked to him when he was little? It clearly no longer did now. For Sawaki, nature had lost its definition even in his reminiscences. Just as nature did not feature in his daily reality, it had gone from his memory too. That was probably why he had never been forced to contemplate suicide, or even felt as sad as Shinkichi Yoshizawa had.

Sawaki decided to take up Toku's offer to stay the night. As he snuggled into the bedding she laid out for him, he asked her, "Is there anything of your son's that I might have as a keepsake?"

Toku promised to look something out for him.

It did not occur to Sawaki to ask for the diary. The desk editor might want it, but Sawaki felt that it should be buried together with the young man's spirit. It belonged to someone who had been able to hear nature's voice. For anyone who had lost that ability, it was nothing more than meaningless words.

The wind blowing in off the sea continued to rattle the roof and the shutters throughout the night.

The next morning, Toku accompanied Sawaki as far as Shari station. The wind was as strong as ever, but it had stopped snowing and the sun had come out. Toku said nothing about the memento as they rode the horse-drawn sled, and Sawaki assumed she had probably been unable to find anything suitable.

Shari station was buried in snow. Just as the day before, nobody was in sight. As he stood on the icy platform with Toku waiting for the train to arrive, Sawaki recalled the toy monkey. He would probably never understand its significance, he thought.

"What happened to that toy monkey?" he asked Toku.

She smiled. "That boy was clutching it right until the end, so I decided to put it in his grave along with the diary."

"Good idea," nodded Sawaki, although secretly he would have liked to have had it as a memento. It would not be of any use for his article, though, since he still did not know why the youth had treasured it.

The train arrived. Just as Sawaki was boarding it, Toku rummaged around in her bag and pulled out a small square package.

"Please take this," she urged Sawaki, passing the cloth-wrapped bundle to him through the window. "When he was little, he used to treasure this. I don't know whether it's a good memento or not, though."

"What is it?"

Toku's reply was drowned out by the train's whistle and Sawaki could not catch it.

After her small body had disappeared from sight, Sawaki closed the window and opened up the package on his knees. It contained a weathered old cardboard box, along with a note written in clumsy handwriting.

My husband, who died young, made this for our boy. He was an only child, and it served as a playmate for him when he was little. It's not much, but please take it.

Sawaki opened up the lid of the box. Inside was a wooden toy monkey. It was clumsily made, clearly fashioned by a novice, but there was a curious charm in its expression.

Sawaki noticed a long string in its back. When he pulled it, the monkey clapped its hands together with a clattering sound, just as that cheap toy had done.

House of Cards

The main street was beginning to stir to the morning, but the dregs of night still hung in the air of the side alley lined with cheap bars and dubious eateries specializing in offal.

For some time now, bright flashes from the forensics photographer's camera had ripped through the darkness, illuminating the prone body of a young woman. She was wearing a trashy sequined dress, and her bare feet were shod with plastic slip-on sandals, one of which lay in the gutter beside her—a hostess from one of the bars, by the looks of her.

Taguchi turned her over. "Bring the light closer, will you?" he called out to his junior, Detective Suzuki.

The circle from the flashlight revealed a flat, featureless face twisted in a grimace of pain. Her thick makeup was grotesque, as if she had applied it to look good when she died.

She had been strangled. Taguchi loosened the thin black ribbon wound tightly around her slim neck, and saw that it was a plain black necktie.

She must be around twenty-two or twenty-three years of age, he thought. Or perhaps the bare face under all that makeup might reveal itself to be a little younger than that. In any case, she had been too young to die.

"Boss!" Suzuki held up a sandal showing Taguchi the sole. "There's a brand name on it," he said excitedly.

In the flashlight Taguchi made out the words "Turkish Sun." He had thought she was a bar hostess, but perhaps she worked at a bathhouse. Not that it made much difference, he thought. Either way she had been at work in the entertainment district, and as such it was not hard to imagine why she had been killed—it must have been either for money or for a man.

"I'll go check it out," said Suzuki, taking off out of the alley like a bloodhound on the scent. It was the twenty-seven-year-old's first murder case since his transfer to Shibuya police station and he was overcompensating for nervousness. So young, thought Taguchi, amused. He had also been like that once—and not all that long ago, either, although now his subordinates called him the Old Fox. Even the Old Fox had once been a bloodhound.

Smiling wryly to himself, he took out a cigarette and lit it. The morning light was finally beginning to filter into the alley, and the woman's cadaver appeared thin and forlorn in the pale light. The murderer would not have needed much strength to kill her, he thought. Averting his eyes, he decided to pay a visit to the nearby police box and hear what the patrolman who discovered the body had to say. As he left the alley, the rear view of his rotund, bandy-legged figure did somehow resemble that of an old fox.

In the afternoon, a fine, dreary drizzle started falling. It was typical rainy season weather, hot and humid. Taguchi hated this time of year. Being overweight did not help—even just standing still, he quickly broke out in a sweat.

"Well?" He wiped the moisture from the back of his neck before looking up at Detective Suzuki. "How did you get on at Turkish Sun?"

"They knew her—they even had a copy of her CV. Here," Suzuki handed him a standard format résumé form folded in half. Taguchi sank back in his swivel chair and opened out it out.

Name	Kazuko Watanabe
Date of Birth	May 7, 1949
Permanent residence	A_____ Village, A_____ County, Tochigi Prefecture
Education	A____ Village Junior High School
Employment	S____ Pharmaceuticals, Shinagawa Factory
	Chat Noir Tearoom
	Shochiku Cabaret

That was it—in barely legible handwriting. It was a pretty familiar scenario, thought Taguchi. A girl from a rural area gets a respectable job in Tokyo through the mass recruitment program. Before long she moves to a tearoom, then to a cabaret, and finally to a bathhouse-cum-brothel. It was a classic descent into degradation, although she probably thought she was moving up in the world.

"The victim appears to have been on the night shift last night," Suzuki said, consulting his notebook.

Taguchi raised his eyes to his subordinate's face. "They have night shifts at a bathhouse?"

"The girls apparently take turns in staying overnight. The manager claims it's a precaution against fire, but—"

"So you reckon the murderer knew she was on the night shift, and called her out to the alley in order to kill her?"

"It narrows the field," Suzuki's eyes glittered. "The victim had gone to the trouble of making herself up before going out, so it's reasonable to assume that she was meeting someone she was pretty close to."

"Were there any men in her life?"

"She was getting married in the fall."

"Ah," Taguchi's eyes widened. This piece of news was unexpected, although not inconceivable for a girl working in a bathhouse. After all, she turned out to be only twenty-one. "Who's the lucky man?"

"The boss of a small workshop. Forty years of age. Widowed. He's a regular at Turkish Sun, and got to know the victim there."

"Were they really planning to get married? It's not just gossip?"

"It seems so. There's a reservation in their names at a nearby wedding hall. And the victim was happily showing off a marriage brochure to the other girls."

"So she was engaged to be married, huh?" Taguchi turned his gaze out of the window. The Tokyo Culture Center and bus terminal looked blurred and hazy through the glass misted with raindrops. When he found out the victim worked in a bathhouse, the dark image of a fallen woman had immediately come to mind. However, what Suzuki came back with was a story of an ordinary twenty-one-year-old girl, her heart aflutter with plans for marriage.

Not only that, but...

With a troubled expression, Taguchi recalled the body lying in the alley. Suzuki had said the girl must have been going to meet a man she was on close terms with, since she had made herself up. That certainly made sense—but if it had indeed been the case, why had she slipped her feet into those scruffy sandals? They were printed with the name of the bathhouse and were provided for the use of customers. If she had gone to the trouble of making herself up for a man, why hadn't she worn some nice smart shoes to go out and meet him?

Perhaps there was more to this case than met the eye?

Taguchi looked pensive for a moment, but quickly recovered his usual smile. The murderer's identity would become clear as the investigation progressed, he thought. Things that looked strange at first glance often turned out to have a perfectly rational explanation when the case was solved. Twenty years' experience as a detective had instilled him with confidence.

He heaved himself out of the chair. "It's about time we paid the workshop boss a visit, don't you think?"

"Yoshimuta Packaging" was inscribed in gold lettering on the glass door. It was not so much a workshop as the front room of an ordinary town house. A small truck was parked outside, the name Yoshimuta Packaging emblazoned on its side. From inside the house, the regular *thwump* of a cutter could be heard.

When Suzuki pressed the doorbell, the sound of the machine stopped, the glass door opened, and a middle-aged man with a growth of stubble on his chin peered out. Dressed in a sleeveless undershirt and long johns, he was broad-chested and sweating profusely. Drying himself with the hand towel slung around his neck, he stared at the two detectives, "What can I do for you?"

Taguchi showed him his police badge. "I guess you haven't heard yet, then?"

"Heard what?" Yoshimuta looked questioningly at the two men as he showed them inside.

Taguchi did not answer at once; instead he glanced around the wooden-floored workspace. It was thirteen or fourteen square meters in size, and equipped with a large cutting machine.

Ready-trimmed posters were piled almost as high as the ceiling, but there was no sign of any employees. It appeared that he worked alone. This really was what you would call a cottage industry, thought Taguchi. The window was open, but not a breath of air came in. He took out his handkerchief and dabbed at the back of his neck.

"About the murder of Kazuko Watanabe of Turkish Sun," Taguchi looked directly into Yoshimuta's eyes, ready to catch any reaction in his expression. "I heard you were due to marry her, is that right?"

"Kazuko? I don't believe it!" Yoshimuta's face crumpled. His hand, still clutching the towel, stopped in mid-air and his shoulders slumped as he groaned, "Who on earth…?"

"That's what we intend to find out," said Taguchi slowly. "Were there any problems with you two getting married?"

"What do you mean? Everyone was really happy for us! We'd sometimes talk about what it was going to be like once we were married. It might sound a bit odd for someone my age, but I was serious about her, you know. And now—"

Taguchi was taken aback to see tears glistening in Yoshimuta's eyes. This big bear of a man was all choked up. Taguchi was surprised, but unmoved. In fact, he was instantly on his guard. It was unfortunate, but so many years working as a detective had made him naturally wary. He had seen any number of criminals feigning tears after having coolly murdered a lover.

He deliberately wiped the back of his neck once more. "Didn't you go to Turkish Sun last night?"

"I wanted to, but I've had a rush job in these past few days." Yoshimuta pointed to the pile of posters still waiting to be trimmed, saying that he would have to work through the night again tonight to meet the deadline. But now he didn't feel like working, he added with a sigh.

"Do you know of any men who were close to Kazuko, other than you?"

After rubbing his eyes with his thick fingers, Yoshimuta answered, "There is one, but he's not the one you're after."

"Who is he?"

"He's called Sakakibara. A young guy who writes poetry."

"Poetry?" echoed Taguchi, puzzled. It was not unthinkable for a bathhouse girl to get together with a local small workshop owner. It even seemed like a pretty good match. But a *poet*? That just didn't add up. "What sort of relationship did she have with this poet?"

"Kazuko had been through a lot, and Sakakibara liked to hear her talk about it. She could tell him all her troubles and he would listen to her. She would say that just talking to him made her feel better about things. Poets are known for their sensitivity, aren't they? Of course, once we decided to get married, she was really happy and didn't have so much to grumble about any more."

"Wasn't this Sakakibara scrounging off her? Sweet-talking her into giving him money, or something like that?"

"If you meet him you'll know he's not that sort. He's clever, but he doesn't brag about it. He's a great guy."

"So where can I meet this great guy?"

"I don't know where he lives, but he often goes to Julie's—that small bar behind the station. That's where I got to know him. Other than that, he sometimes sells his poetry books outside Shibuya station, by Hachiko. They go for fifty yen. I bought one once, but I can't say I understood much of it."

So it was that guy who sold poetry. Taguchi recalled having seen him several times by the Hachiko statue. He was tall and thin, and vaguely hippyish, although Taguchi's memory of him was hazy, having seen him only in passing. In any case, he would just have to meet him to get an idea of the sort of man he was.

Taguchi asked Yoshimuta one last question, "Did you work all night last night too?"

Yoshimuta answered slowly, "Pretty much—although I did get two or three hours shut-eye in that chair over there."

Taguchi sent Detective Suzuki back to Turkish Sun before setting off alone for Julie's, the bar that Yoshimuta had told him about.

It was on the corner of the very alley where the body had been found; small, with a sign on the door reading "No Under-18s by Law." Taguchi could not help a wry smile as he went in.

There were just two customers in the small, dimly lit interior. One was at the counter, an older man with a neat little mustache who was intent on teasing the landlady. Glancing over at the other, much younger man, Taguchi had the feeling he had seen him before somewhere. He had long hair and a beard, and was seated at a table in the corner toying with his glass, now half empty. On the table before him lay a red leather-bound book. Taguchi went up to him and, having noted the title *Selected Poems of Baudelaire* on the spine, took a seat in front of him.

"You must be Sakakibara."

The young man looked up, his face unhealthily pale in the semi-darkness. There was a trace of amusement in his eyes as he nodded.

"I'm from the Shibuya Police Sta—"

"I could tell you were a detective from a mile off," interrupted Sakakibara. "Police all have a distinctive smell."

"Is that so? I hadn't noticed personally."

"A dung beetle rooting around in shit doesn't notice how much it stinks."

"You don't seem too fond of the police."

"Can't say I am. They make out they're on the side of justice, but what they call justice is synonymous with the Establishment. The moment you do anything antiestablishment, they immediately crack down on you in the name of justice. I joined a protest against the US–Japan Security Treaty and was locked up for a week."

"I see," laughed Taguchi.

Sakakibara sneered. "I don't want your rotten sympathy. Why don't you get on and question me about that girl who was killed. That's what you came for, isn't it?"

"I guess so." Taguchi turned toward the counter and ordered a beer, his brows knotted in a frown. By the time his gaze returned to the young man, however, his amicable smile was once again in place. "Now that I've met you, I find I'm just as interested in you as I am in the case."

"How so?"

"I've been a detective for twenty years. If you'll allow me to speak from long experience, sarcastic people like you are surprisingly submissive deep down. You're ashamed of it, so you hide behind a mask of sarcasm and make yourself out to be the villain."

"Are you saying I'm submissive?" Sakakibara gave a brief chuckle. It was a nervous, feminine sort of laugh, noted Taguchi, which matched the gentle-looking long, slender fingers wrapped around his glass.

"Is that all your twenty years of experience has taught you? What a shallow way of seeing things." Sakakibara snickered. "People are more complicated than that. You can't just explain them away as neatly as that. If you approach this girl's murder with such a simplistic mindset, you'll never catch the culprit."

"Sounds like you know who did it." Taguchi leaned forward in his chair and looked searchingly at the young man. The collar of his purple shirt afforded a peek of shallow chest. His lips were thin, too. He really did look somewhat neurotic—and sensitive, although there was also something cold about him.

Sakakibara put down his glass, and took a crumpled cigarette out of his shirt pocket, slowly straightened it out, and put it in his mouth.

"I wouldn't say I know who did it, but I am familiar with the case."

Taguchi raised his beer to his mouth. It was barely chilled, and unappetizing.

"We've also learned a few things about the case." Taguchi put the beer down. "The bathhouse girl who was strangled to death— her name was Kazuko Watanabe. She was twenty-one years of age. She was on the night shift. There were two men in her life: one was a workshop owner she was due to marry; the other was you. Is there anything else I should know?"

"Yes. The very crux of the matter."

"Ah."

"Do you know what the key to solving a murder case is?" Sakakibara looked defiantly at him. Taguchi had to smile. This youngster seriously appeared to be lecturing him, a detective with twenty years' experience, on the basic rules of solving a crime. It was just as well young Suzuki wasn't here. He would have been apoplectic with rage by now. "The motive." Sakakibara stubbed out his cigarette in the ashtray.

"The motive?" Taguchi laughed. "Even a child knows that."

"But you lot don't know what that really means. If someone gets stabbed, then there must be a subtle difference between a case where a woman crazed with jealousy stabs a man, and one where a lunatic stabs someone for no reason. With the former, there must be hatred involved, and even love, too. But you detectives don't understand that subtle difference. Strangulation is just that, strangulation to you. And you don't even realize that you're missing the essence of the crime."

"So, what do you reckon is the motive in this case?"

"There is no motive. That's the distinguishing feature of this case." Sakakibara grinned, pleased with himself.

"No motive?" queried Taguchi, tonelessly.

"That's right. If the motive reveals the killer's face, then in this case there is no face. So you guys will never catch the murderer."

"We'll see about that."

"I had to laugh."

"If you're trying to wind me up, it's not going to work. You're just an amateur."

"And I won't be able to stop laughing. Especially if you don't get him, and the press criticize you for incompetence."

"I'm grateful for your concern, but shouldn't you be more worried for yourself?"

"Are you saying I'm on your list of suspects?"

"Not just you."

"Me and the workshop owner, then?"

"I met him earlier."

"So you've been wasting your time." Sakakibara snickered again. "That man couldn't even harm a fly. He hasn't got the guts to do something like that, or the motive. He really wanted to marry her, you know."

"So what about you?"

"It'd be great if I had a motive, but I'm afraid I don't."

"You had a thing for her, didn't you?"

"That's just the sort of crude comment I'd expect from a detective," Sakakibara shrugged. "But yes, I did like her. Not in the vulgar way you're imagining, though, but in a poetic, spiritual sense."

"Poetic?"

"You heard. But it wasn't just her—I like all the bargirls in this alley. All of them are burdened with misfortune, yet they're gentle and sweet. They're much more womanly than those pretentious celebrities or girls from rich families. I get them to tell me about themselves, and in return I dedicate one of my clumsy poems to them. Did you know that Baudelaire spoke of woman as slave to the muse, and the poet as slave to woman?"

"Meaning they're mutually dependent on one another, I suppose?"

Sakakibara muttered something under his breath, but it sounded like French and Taguchi could not understand. He was probably cursing Taguchi's vulgar language as unworthy of the muse.

Taguchi's silence seemed to restore Sakakibara's good mood. "Shall I tell you something else you don't know?" he asked, a smile playing around his lips. "She had almost two million yen in the bank."

Seeing the gleam in Taguchi's eyes, Sakakibara grinned. "I suppose you're thinking that two million yen is motive enough for murder, but it merely serves to prove mine and Yoshimuta's innocence."

"How's that?"

"She always used to say that out of those two million, she would give one and a half million to her husband once they were married, as capital for his business. The remaining half million was for penniless little me, to pay the costs of publishing an edition of my poetry. Everyone knew about it. Now that she's been killed, far from profiting from her death, Yoshimuta and I have lost out on our share of those two million yen. In other words, those two million in the bank indirectly prove our innocence. That'll stump the police now, won't it? I sympathize. Looking at the situation on the ground, the murderer has to be a man close to her. There are only two men close to her, Yoshimuta and me. But as I just said, neither of us have a motive. So now do you understand what I meant by a crime with neither a face nor a motive?"

"Where do you get money to live on?"

"Huh?"

A flicker of dismay ran across Sakakibara's self-satisfied expression, and his pallid face reddened at Taguchi's unexpected query. "I've been talking about things that are crucial to your investigation, so why do you come out with something trivial like that?

"Looks like I've upset you," laughed Taguchi. "I asked because I'm concerned about you. You want to publish a collection of poetry, but you haven't got any money, right? Yet you're a regular at this bar. So you've got enough money for that, I guess."

"I work for money, in my own way. I sell copies of my poems, and I make money at Pachinko. And when I haven't got any money, I don't drink. I don't like drudgery. Idleness is the mark of a free man, after all."

"A free man?" Taguchi gave a sardonic smile as he rose to his feet. "I expect I'll want to talk to you again. May I have your address?"

When Taguchi arrived back at the office, Suzuki was already there. "You look tired," he commented with some concern.

"Yup. I'm on my last legs," smiled Taguchi, before wiping his face with the towel Suzuki held out to him. The day was as clammy as ever. "So did you find out any more?"

"The victim had almost two million deposited in a local bank. It seemed she managed to save that much in just a year, so being a bathhouse girl isn't such a bad business."

"I've heard some girls manage to put by fifteen million in the space of five years," laughed Taguchi. "I heard about her savings from that poet Sakakibara. Who's going to get it now she's dead?"

"Her parents are still alive, so I suppose it'll go to them. The other girls at the bathhouse told me that Sakakibara was poor so she planned to give him half a million so he could publish a collection of poetry. The remaining million and a half was for Yoshimuta's business once they were married. Apparently she often used to talk about it."

"Yes, I already heard about it from Sakakibara. So apart from Yoshimuta and Sakakibara, wasn't there any other guy she was on intimate terms with?"

"I made a point of asking about that too, but it seems there wasn't anyone else. A year or so ago there was some cheap gangster type giving her a certain amount of bother, but three months ago he was killed in a fight with another yakuza."

"Which just leaves those two." Taguchi sank back in his chair and folded his arms. Behind him, an electric fan squeaked gloomily, evidently in need of oil. It was merely stirring up the hot air in the room to little effect. Irritated by the noise, Taguchi turned it off.

So, which of the two men was the murderer? Was it the middle-aged workshop owner, or the young self-styled poet?

Sakakibara had exultantly claimed this was a crime with no motive. It was true that at this moment in time no obvious motive had presented itself. But Taguchi could not believe there was any such thing as a crime with no motive. Many murderers did act on impulse, but something must have led them to do it. If someone committed a crime, there had to be a motive. The fact that there did not appear to be one only meant that they had not yet discovered it.

"What's Sakakibara like?" asked Suzuki.

Taguchi turned the fan back on. "He talks too much. He told me he doesn't like the police. I suppose it's because he was arrested at an anti-Security Treaty demo and locked up for a week. Ah, right, would you check that he really was detained?"

"Has it got anything to do with the murder?"

"Probably not. I just want to know as much as I can about him."

"I'll call HQ."

After Suzuki had left the room, Taguchi rose from his chair and gazed out of the window. The neon lights of the entertainment district were stunning. Sakakibara was probably still comfortably installed in that bar and no doubt enjoying poking fun at the police. Taguchi chuckled to himself. Sakakibara probably thought he had won the first round, but Taguchi merely considered his behavior childish. The kid would sooner or later find out how frightening the police could be. And he would regret having ever tried to mess with them.

Suzuki was back in twenty minutes.

"Sakakibara was indeed arrested the day of that demo and detained at Kamata police station. But..."

"But what?"

"He wasn't arrested for attending the demo. He was arrested for shoplifting. Books."

"Hmm, was he now?"

Taguchi grew pensive, recalling Sakakibara's pale face. Why had he lied? Perhaps it sounded cooler to say you had been arrested at a demo, rather than for shoplifting? Whatever the reason, Taguchi felt that this trivial incident was somehow revealing of the young man's character.

The following afternoon, the results of the autopsy came through. The cause of death was suffocation by strangulation with a necktie, a cheap, commonplace article on which no fingerprints could be detected. The time of death was a simple matter, estimated at between two and three o'clock in the morning.

Suzuki had gone to investigate Yoshimuta's alibi, while Taguchi headed out in the rain, which as bad luck would have had just started, to meet Sakakibara.

As he arrived at the Peace Villa apartment block, it started to really pelt down. Even for the rainy season, this was a serious downpour. The block was a flimsily constructed, run-of-the-mill mortared wood-frame building with cracks stained dark from the rain running through its walls. It was so close to the building next door they were almost touching, and as Taguchi went in, he was enveloped in shadowy semi-darkness even though it was only five in the afternoon.

After stopping to check the room number with the caretaker, Taguchi climbed the creaking staircase to the second floor. It was the last door at the end of the corridor, upon which the sign "Contemporary Poetry Appreciation Society" written in large letters had been stuck in place of a nameplate.

Contemporary Poetry Appreciation Society...? Taguchi felt the young man had bitten off rather more than he could chew.

When he knocked on the door, a young woman peered out. She was not wearing any makeup, but she was clearly a bargirl. As soon as she realized Taguchi was a detective, she turned and called into the room, "Sensei, it's the police here to see you."

Sakakibara, naked from the waist up, was lying on a pile of unmade bedding in the corner of the tiny room staring up at the ceiling. His hippyish beard stood out starkly against his hollow chest. As Taguchi stepped into the room, he raised himself sluggishly and said in a sleepy voice, "Ah, come in, come in!"

The girl stood by the door looking from one to the other, and then took her leave telling Sakakibara in a low voice, "It's about time to go to work, so…"

"She's a hostess at Julie's," Sakakibara said, pushing an ashtray over to Taguchi. "She lives next door, but she sometimes comes over to cook dinner for me or to have a chat."

"I don't remember her being at the bar last night."

"She'd taken the night off. Hostesses may look like they're having fun, but in reality it's hard work. If they're feeling tired, they're usually told to go home. Nobody's going to look after them if they fall ill, after all."

"She's the sort of sweet girl you were talking about, right?"

"That's right," nodded Sakakibara, flinging the window wide open. The gray wall of the building next door was close enough to touch, preventing much of a breeze from coming in. Instead, they were sprayed with rain.

Sakakibara tutted in irritation and closed the window again. "She's a nice girl. She's suffered so much hardship, but she's always surprisingly cheerful. And even if her talk is a bit coarse, deep down she's simple-hearted, childlike even."

"Sounds pretty angelic, coming from you," said Taguchi somewhat sarcastically.

Sakakibara frowned. "You don't understand," he retorted. "You lot judge people only by their job title. As far as you're concerned, the only people innocent of wrongdoing are ministers or the bosses of big companies. On the other hand, if you come across a bargirl or a tramp, you're immediately under the illusion that they have a sinister criminal feel about them. You'll never be able to understand how magnificent they are."

"Meaning that you do, I suppose."

"Of course. I possess a free spirit. It was only the obscure poets and painters who saw the heart of an angel in the whores of Paris's Montparnasse." His face flushed with triumph, Sakakibara went on to list the names of French artists Taguchi had never heard of.

"This sort of talk is beyond me," grimaced Taguchi. "Today I've come to see if I can get you to recall where you were yesterday between two and three in the morning. How about it?"

"My alibi, you mean?" Sakakibara shrugged. "I work at night. All I can tell you is that I was alone writing poetry. Writing is solitary work, so of course I don't have anyone to back me up. I suppose that, in your words, I don't have an alibi."

"Not so much that you don't have one, but it's rather weak, I'd say," Taguchi reassured him, then glanced around the room. It was small, and the unmade bed and lack of a view made it seem all the more cramped. It was a tiny room that reeked of poverty. There was a small desk facing the wall, upon which was placed a mimeograph stencil; a disordered heap of magazines and manuscript paper; underwear hung up to dry on a bit of string attached to the ceiling. It was a far cry from the bombast of the sign proclaiming the Contemporary Poetry Appreciation Society.

"You said you sold collections of your poetry, right?"

"I don't suppose you'd like to purchase one?"

"Yes, if you've one to spare?"

"I never expected to come across a detective interested in contemporary poetry," commented Sakakibara sarcastically, before taking down a book from the shelf and placing it in front of him.

It was a flimsy mimeographed copy, with "The Poetry of Tetsuya Sakakibara, published by the Contemporary Poetry Appreciation Society" printed on the cover. Noting the price on the back, Taguchi placed a fifty-yen coin next to the ashtray.

The last page featured a brief résumé of the author. Taguchi had just noted the birth date of 1942, realizing that made Sakakibara twenty-seven, the same age as Detective Suzuki, when the caretaker came upstairs to inform him of a telephone call.

The call was from Suzuki, who had gone to check up on Yoshimuta's alibi. As Taguchi picked up the receiver, his agitated voice came rushing out, "Yoshimuta's been run over."

"Is he dead?" Involuntarily, Taguchi raised his voice.

"He's in hospital, but the doctors don't hold much hope."

Suzuki gave him the name of the hospital. Senselessly, Taguchi rubbed the back of his neck with his hand. "What the hell happened?"

"I'm not really sure. I was in the middle of questioning him when his face suddenly drained of color and he ran straight out of the house and into the road and—"

"And was hit by a car?"

"Yes. It was all so sudden I couldn't do anything about it."

"Okay, I'm on my way." Taguchi replaced the receiver and turned round to find Sakakibara standing there behind him.

"Has something happened?"

"Are you worried?" spat Taguchi.

"Not especially." Sakakibara's lip curled as he turned his back.

Taguchi observed him climb back upstairs, limping. His expression hardened. He had not noticed it before, but Sakakibara was clearly dragging his left leg behind him.

By the time Taguchi arrived at the hospital, the owner of Yoshimuta Packaging was already dead. Detective Suzuki was white as a sheet, and apologized as if it was his personal responsibility. Taguchi clapped him on the back and told him he was not to blame.

"More to the point, did he say anything before he died?"

"In the ambulance on the way here he just kept repeating that he hadn't killed her. That's all he said."

"So what do you think?"

"When he suddenly ran off like that I thought he must be guilty, but now I don't think he was."

"Because of what he said? There are people who tell lies on their deathbed, you know."

"Of course I don't think he's innocent just because of what he said. There's another reason."

"Which is?"

"I found out he was headed for bankruptcy. His workshop was mortgaged, and he had loans amounting to almost a million yen. In other words, he really needed that million and a half yen from the victim."

"I suppose he, of all people, would have known that he would get that money when they married, but he wouldn't get anything if she died."

"That's right. And what's more, the victim had told him right from the start that she wanted the money to be capital for his business, so he had no need to kill her anyway. Even if we concede that he was only after her money, surely he would have married her and got his hands on the money before killing her?"

"I see," nodded Taguchi. He recalled Yoshimuta's face when they had gone to see him in his matchbox of a workshop to inform him of Kazuko Watanabe's death. He had been so upset that he wept. At the time, Taguchi had been astonished to see the tears well up in his eyes, but in hindsight it had probably been less due to his grief over having lost his girl, as his utter despair at the inevitable bankruptcy he faced having lost that million and a half yen. It was unlikely a grown man like him would have been moved to tears merely on hearing his fiancée had just died. But Yoshimuta's livelihood had been staked on this marriage.

"So the reason he ran out in front of a car is also clear, isn't it? It was obviously suicide. It's not your fault."

"I hope not, but..." A trace of self-reproach remained in Suzuki's face. He was young, and somebody had just died before his eyes—it would not be easy to recover from such a shock. The best way to help him to get over it would be either to take him off the case altogether and force him to rest, or alternatively to keep him on the case and work him to the bone.

Considering Suzuki's youth, Taguchi decided on the latter course. It was by far the better plan to send a young bloodhound off in pursuit of a quarry.

"There's no need to worry about Yoshimuta any longer," he asserted in a deliberately forceful voice. "In fact, now that he's out of the way, we've got our rat."

"You mean Sakakibara?"

"That's right. The trail's gone cold on Yoshimuta, which leaves just him. He's so damn cocksure that we'll never get him, but I'm gonna nail him. I want you to stake out his apartment."

Taguchi patted Suzuki on the shoulder and ushered him out of the room, then he too went out. It was still raining. As he walked to the alley where the murder had taken place, Taguchi visualized Sakakibara's face and started talking to him. *You're on your own now. You can't hide behind that grown man Yoshimuta any longer. I'll smoke you out of your hole in no time.*

The alley was sodden with rain. As always it stank of booze and cooked offal. The squeals of women and raucous bellows of customers spilled out of the bars and drinking houses; drunken men getting wet in the rain bawled out war songs as they reeled past Taguchi. It hardly seemed possible that just yesterday a young woman's body had lain here. But it had, and the murderer was still wandering around free.

Taguchi pushed open the door to Julie's and went in. Luckily there were no customers, and the hostess he had met at Sakakibara's was leaning on the counter, her chin resting on her hands, and she looked bored. "You're the detective, right?" She introduced herself as Mineko Igarashi, but wariness showed in her eyes.

"I'd like to ask you about Sakakibara." When he said this, her expression became even more guarded.

"What would you like to know about Sensei?"

"Why do you call him Sensei? Are you learning about poetry from him?"

"I don't know anything about poetry. But I respect him—that's why. Anything wrong with that?"

"Did Kazuko Watanabe, the girl who was murdered, call him Sensei too?"

"Yeah, sure."

"What does he do for you girls?"

"He's a good listener and gives us advice."

"What can he do? He doesn't have any money or influence, does he? You say he gives you advice, but all he can really do is listen, right?"

"That's enough for us."

"Really? That's enough?" Taguchi just didn't get it. If it was simply a matter of listening to their woes, wouldn't their drunken customers do just as well?

When he suggested as much to her, she retorted scornfully, "You haven't got a clue, have you? The customers here are only interested in hearing about our lives for the fun of it. Either that, or they pretend to sympathize in order to get close to us. You can see from the start they've got an ulterior motive. But Sensei's not like that. He really listens to us. Who wouldn't want a friend like that?"

"You don't think he's putting on an act?"

"An act?" Mineko tilted her head to one side. She was no beauty, and perhaps that was what made her look very young. In some respects she looked terribly grown-up, but somewhere in her heart she had been hurt. If you made out you were soothing over that wound, it would probably be easy to deceive such a woman.

"Don't you think he just sympathizes with you so as to give a good impression of himself, when in fact he really despises you?"

"No, he's not the type," she said hotly.

"Have you any proof of that?" prodded Taguchi nastily. When Mineko retorted that she did, his eyes widened. "What sort of proof?"

"A while back, Kazuko was being stalked by some yakuza lowlife. Everyone was too scared to stick up for her, but Sensei went to her aid and stood up to him."

"What happened?"

"Sensei's no match for a guy like that. He got a thrashing, but the yakuza was arrested. Thanks to him, Kazu was safe. That really got to me! Anyone just putting on an act couldn't possibly do anything like that. He could have gotten himself killed!"

As she talked, her wariness of Taguchi melted away and she started enthusing about how compassionate Sakakibara was. "And that's not all. Sensei's got a bad leg, you know that, right?"

"I'd noticed."

"He got that from saving a child about to be run over by a car, a child he'd never even seen before!"

"Did you see it happen?"

"No, but I heard about it from Sensei's friend who came over to the apartment."

"And you believed him?"

"Of course. He's famous, after all. You've heard of Kyo Sasanuma, haven't you?"

Taguchi nodded. He was a popular young author. Taguchi had even read his short story "One Debauched Morning" in a magazine. He could still recall the strangely upbeat account of a top executive being drawn into a world of sex and gambling. A subject once considered degenerate had been converted into an adventure, and Taguchi had found it quite thought-provoking.

"It was him," Mineko said proudly. It was as if she thought that just having such a famous friend conferred status on Sakakibara himself. Taguchi was amused by her naïveté, but said nothing. "So if the police think Sensei's the murderer, they're making a big mistake," she added conclusively.

"Maybe," replied Taguchi noncommittally.

Mineko was evidently devoted to Sakakibara. She appeared entirely unembarrassed by her absolute belief in him.

Taguchi believed only facts. Yet it was also the facts that troubled him. Mineko had witnessed how Sakakibara had stood up to the yakuza to save Kazuko, so that was probably a fact. There was a strong possibility that what she had said about him saving a child was also a fact. The image of Sakakibara that such facts conjured just did not fit with the image of him that Taguchi had created in his mind over the past two days. The Sakakibara that carried a collection of Baudelaire's poetry even when going to a bar to drink; who hung the pompous sign "Contemporary Poetry Appreciation Society" on the door of his room in that rundown apartment block; and who lied that he had been detained at a demonstration when actually he had been arrested for shoplifting: these three facts described a young man who was the very picture of vanity. It did not seem possible to square this image of Sakakibara with Mineko's depiction of him.

And then there was also another image: that of Sakakibara the murderer.

How on earth could these three profiles fit together?

I guess establishing the motive is going to be the key to this case...

The following afternoon, after first confirming by telephone, Taguchi visited Kyo Sasanuma at his home in the exclusive Aoyama district. He lived in a twelve-story upmarket condominium, but his compact two-bedroom condo was a far cry from the sumptuous lifestyle Taguchi had imagined from the author's work.

Sasanuma looked sleepy, as if he had been working through the night. To Taguchi's query, he replied dryly, "Sakakibara and I studied French literature together at university. We often stayed up all night discussing it. Has he done something wrong?"

"I just want to know what sort of person he is. Tetsuya Sakakibara, that is. I guess you would know?"

"Depends what you mean by 'know,' really. Some would say it's impossible to understand another person." Sasanuma gave a short laugh.

"I suppose." Taguchi did not resist. Instead he tried another tack. "Is it true that he was hit by a car while saving a child?"

"Yes, it's true. It was in our fourth year at university. Sakakibara, myself, and another guy I'll call 'N' were walking along when a kid of three or four ran out into the street. A truck was coming from the opposite direction. At times like that your brain tells you that you have to save the kid from danger, but your body doesn't react. Of course, you also feel fear. But Sakakibara never hesitated for a moment. He saved the kid, but he got his left leg injured."

"Is he brave?"

"Sure. At least, I couldn't do what he did. I always put myself first, I'm afraid. I'm too much of a snob."

"But you're a popular author, while he's an unknown poet who has to sell cheap fifty-yen collections of his work on the street just to eat. The way I see it, you're a winner and he's a loser."

"That's because we live in a complicated age. I myself really can't say who is the winner and who is the loser. For all I know, he might be the winner. There are times I long for his way of life. I get the feeling that he's free, and to be free you have to be true to yourself."

"*Is* he true to himself?" A shadow of irony flashed across Taguchi's eyes.

Sasanuma was quick to note this and, looking rather puzzled, he commented, "It seems you have a rather different view of him."

"If I'm honest, yes I do. But that aside, may I ask you to explain in what way Sakakibara is true to himself?"

"Hmm, let me think," Sasanuma folded his arms and thought a while. "Not long ago he was arrested at a demonstration against the US–Japan Security Treaty. It's not just that he's anti-establishment, he happens to have the honesty to translate it into action. I, on the other hand, might be daring in my novels, but in real life I'm the very picture of conservatism."

"Did he tell you he had been at the demo?"

"Yes. In fact, when he was released I went to Kamata police station to pick him up. I developed a bit of a complex about it at the time. He later wrote a poem about the demo. It's a great poem."

Still seated, Sasanuma reached out and took a familiar-looking mimeographed poetry collection off his desk. Opening it up to a page near the middle, he said, "The title is 'The Flash.' It's a little reminiscent of the Resistance poetry of the French poet Éluard. It's really a masterpiece."

Taguchi had never heard of Éluard. But he did know that Sakakibara had lied, and had written a poem about a demonstration he had never been to.

"If I told you it was a lie, what would you think?"

"A lie?"

"What if he hadn't been at that demo? For example, if he had been arrested for some other crime such as theft, yet had lied to you that he had been arrested at the demonstration? What would you make of that?"

"Don't be ridiculous," Sasanuma gave a tight smile. "Surely he has no need to lie about something like that. I'm just some half-baked minor celebrity so I have to consider my position. I have to put on a show to sell myself. Making subversive comments, in my case, is just a publicity stunt. But he's different. He isn't afraid of anything. There's no need for him to lie."

There was no trace of irony in his voice. Taguchi did not refer to the demo again, and changed the subject. "Do you think he's capable of murder?"

Naturally, he was not expecting Sasanuma to answer in the affirmative, but he was hoping to get some kind of clue to Sakakibara's nature in his answer.

"Sakakibara capable of murder?" repeated Sasanuma, and then burst out laughing. "I can easily imagine him helping someone. But *killing* someone? No, it really doesn't fit."

"That's the Tetsuya Sakakibara that you know."

"Is there another, different Tetsuya Sakakibara?"

"I reckon there might well be." Taguchi glanced at the book of poetry on the table.

He pictured the tiny, airless room; the mimeographed poetry collections that sold for fifty yen; the grubby, unmade bed—this was the environment Sakakibara lived in. For anyone with a modicum of ambition, such a living must be unbearable. Every day must be a series of humiliations.

The telephone rang. Sasanuma nodded briefly to Taguchi before picking up the receiver. It appeared to be about a piece he was writing for a magazine, for he laughed and said, "I'm thinking of going to Bangkok tomorrow to research it."

Taguchi felt a buzz in the air, utterly unlike the mood in Sakakibara's room. There was not even a phone there. Even if there had been, he was unlikely to receive any calls from magazines asking him to write for them.

Taguchi was just walking into his office, when a call came from Detective Suzuki.

"Sakakibara's right by Hachiko," said Suzuki. The bustle of the street was audible through the receiver. "He's been here for almost an hour now, selling his poetry books. Well, he's just standing there in silence holding a cardboard box with a sign saying, 'Please buy a book of my poems.'"

"Has he sold any?"

"Just one in the last hour. The kid who bought it looked as though he was still in high school. So what now?"

"Um," Taguchi glanced at his watch, the receiver still tucked against his ear. It was just after four. Sakakibara would probably be there for a little longer. Taguchi decided he wanted to see what he looked like as he stood there. "I'm on my way over," he said, hanging up.

The overcast sky still threatened rain, but the area around Hachiko was thronged with the usual young crowd. Taguchi entered the police box by the station where Suzuki was waiting.

Suzuki glanced out through the glass window towards Hachiko, and murmured to Taguchi, "He's still out there."

Sakakibara's skinny figure was visible in the stream of people. He was simply standing there hugging his box of books. Every now and again, he took out a handkerchief and wiped the sweat from his face. Hardly anyone paused before him. A group of three schoolgirls walked past, and then turned around whispering something amongst themselves, but in the end they made no move to buy one.

Shibuya was a well-known hangout for young people, and there was a swirl of energy around Hachiko. Sakakibara alone appeared left behind. He looked not so much lonely as somewhat forlorn and plaintive.

Taguchi took the book he had bought from Sakakibara and placed it before Suzuki. "Want a look?"

"I don't understand poetry!" Suzuki scratched his head, then suddenly his expression turned serious. "Can't we arrest him?" He looked at Taguchi. "He has to be the murderer, right?"

"Right. He is the murderer," agreed Taguchi calmly. "But we don't have any proof."

"But surely he hasn't got an alibi?"

"Yoshimuta didn't have an alibi either, did he? And what's more, if we arrest him now, there are plenty of witnesses ready to testify in his favor. Everybody and his uncle seems to believe he's a great guy. We haven't a hope of winning. The biggest problem is a motive. Right now, we still don't know why he killed Kazuko Watanabe."

"Perhaps he was in love with her? Then she went and told him she was marrying someone else, so—"

"No, no," Taguchi shook his head. Sakakibara was still standing there vacantly. How many would he sell in a day like that? "I thought of that. But if there had been anything like between them, we would have got at least a hint of it during our investigations. But there's been nothing. It's like he said, to him the victim was just another girl who deserved to be loved, nothing more. That's why he bragged to me that it was a crime without a motive. Hang on—"

"What is it?"

"Why did he harp on about the motive?"

"Didn't he say there wasn't a motive?"

"Same difference. He was concerned about the motive. Why was that?"

"If we discover what his motive was, we'll arrest him. Perhaps he was scared of that?"

"That's what I thought. But it's not that. He isn't scared of being arrested, but he is extremely afraid of the motive being discovered. That's why he's so concerned about it."

"I don't understand."

"Let me put it like this. It's a pretty special motive that would utterly disgrace him if it ever became known. Now that would explain his actions, but—"

Suddenly a disturbance broke out in the vicinity of Hachiko.

It was a fight.

A couple of youths were shoving and poking a man of around sixty years old. It seemed the older man had knocked one of them on the shoulder, and they were using this as the pretext for a quarrel.

Passersby had formed a wide circle around the three, but nobody made any move to intervene. The old man himself looked grubby and rather sly, hardly the type to attract sympathy, while the youths both looked like yakuza hoodlums in their sunglasses and sandals.

Taguchi and Suzuki immediately rushed out of the police box, but just as they reached the crowd Taguchi held Suzuki back, "Wait a moment."

"What's up?"

"I want to see what Sakakibara does."

According to Mineko, Sakakibara had been beaten up when he had tried to help Kazuko when she was being stalked. And Sasanuma had told him how Sakakibara had injured his leg trying to save a child from being run over. These two incidents conjured an image of a righteous person incapable of standing back and watching someone else's misfortune. They had even claimed he was incapable of murder. But Taguchi had not witnessed either of those incidents himself.

Therefore, he wanted to make sure with his own eyes. If Sakakibara really was a righteous person, surely he would not be able to ignore this old man being roughed up by a couple of hoodlums?

Taguchi observed Sakakibara over the shoulders of the crowd.

Sakakibara was watching the quarrel. He looked worried. He frowned, sighed and looked away, then looked back. He seemed to be struggling with an invisible force.

"How about an apology, huh?" demanded one of the thugs, roughly shoving the old man's shoulder. The old man staggered and fell heavily onto his buttocks. The other one grabbed his collar and pulled him up again.

"You too old to know how to say sorry?" He gave the old man a resounding slap on the cheek.

The old man made no attempt to defend himself, repeating over and over again, "Sorry! I'm sorry."

· The color drained from Sakakibara's face. His expression was pained, as if he was personally to blame for the old man's beating. The first one punched the old man again.

"Let's break it up!" yelled Suzuki in Taguchi's ear, as if he could not bear it any longer. Just at that moment, Sakakibara laid his cardboard box to one side, and slowly entered the fight circle. Skinny and dragging his left leg, he was not at all a heroic figure.

Going up to the pair, he said, "Cut it out" in a shaky voice. He was clearly terrified. Even so, he was trying to stop the fight.

The pair glared at him. "What have we here?" grinned one.

"Stop bullying the old man."

"Asshole!" The other one suddenly kicked Sakakibara's butt from behind, with the agility of a habitual fighter. As he fell, the other one laid into him. It was a rout. Sakakibara just curled himself up into a fetal position.

So they'd been right about him?

Taguchi felt more and more puzzled. Was Sakakibara really such a righteous person? If he was—

"*Boss!* We've got to stop them!"

At Suzuki's words Taguchi snapped out of it and, yelling, "Stop that right now!" charged his stocky body through the crowd.

Sakakibara was so severely bruised that Taguchi took him to a nearby hospital.

The doctor who examined him diagnosed cracked ribs and ordered him to remain immobile, but lying there in bed Sakakibara was surprisingly cheerful.

"That's a strange face you're making," he said, looking up at Taguchi. "I suppose you're shocked I would do something like that."

"Not particularly."

"You're lying," Sakakibara gave him a searching look. "You're puzzled. And you think this is all an act. You think I made a show of helping that old man because knew I was being tailed. You think a vicious murderer wouldn't do anything to help anyone, don't you?"

Taguchi merely laughed. Sakakibara seemed drunk on his own words. Nodding to himself, he continued, "But unfortunately it wasn't an act. I helped him because I had to. It had nothing to do with whether you were following me or not. When I see something like that, I simply can't ignore it. I'm not particularly proud of myself for having saved him. On the contrary, I'm embarrassed by it."

"I know."

"What the hell do you know? Nothing, that's what."

"It's true that I was puzzled to begin with."

"Surprisingly candid of you."

"But not now. I've been trying to understand you. At first glance, you seem complicated, but actually you're simply a type."

"Now you're lecturing me in anthropology?"

"No, more like my own experiential philosophy. When you went to break up the fight, you were so scared you were shaking."

"So? What are you trying to say?" Sakakibara's expression hardened. "Well, you're right—I am a coward. A total wimp. Anything wrong with that?"

"No," smiled Taguchi. After asking permission to smoke, he lit up a cigarette. "I'm a coward too. But normal people don't try to help if they're scared. At most, they would just call the police, but you steamed in to help even though you were shaking with fear."

"Are you saying I shouldn't have done it?"

"No, that's not what I'm saying. I'm talking about your character. You've got a pretty fascinating personality. You seem to be in thrall to a sense of duty. Today, too, you were bound to help the old man through a sense of obligation. You even seem obsessed with that duty. People usually run away when they're afraid, but you charge in to help because you're afraid."

"What an interesting opinion you have, far more intriguing than a university lecture."

"At worst, it gets to the point that you even lie to deceive yourself and other people. No doubt you believe that poets have to have an anti-establishment mindset. Or perhaps I should say, you're in thrall to that belief. You felt you had a duty to oppose the Security Treaty. But in fact, the day of that demo you were arrested for shoplifting—how mortifying! The normal thing would have been to keep quiet about it, but you went overboard with that sense of duty and lied that you had been at the demo. Not only that, you even wrote a poem about your experience. Otherwise, you wouldn't have been able to live with yourself."

Sakakibara reddened. It seemed Taguchi had hit him where it most hurt. Taguchi slowly stubbed his cigarette out in the ashtray. "So what do you think? Maybe it wasn't such an interesting talk?"

"What the hell are you on about?" Sakakibara chewed his lip and glared at Taguchi. Taguchi smiled.

"I just wanted to get you to confess. You're so full of yourself, defying the police to arrest you. But we will get you. And what's more, your own personality will prove fatal to you. You'll be the cause of your own downfall."

"Ridiculous!" Sakakibara laughed awkwardly. Just at that moment, the door opened and some newspaper reporters barged noisily in.

"Are you the one who stood up to the thugs in the street?" asked one of them, peering at Sakakibara in bed.

Taguchi was called up to the Chief's office. As he went in he saw a newspaper spread out on the desk.

"You read this, I suppose?" A worried expression hovered on the Chief's face as he peered at Taguchi over the top of his glasses.

"Yes, I read it." Taguchi smiled. "All the papers are giving him the hero's treatment. I suppose the fact that it happened during the campaign to banish violence had something to do with it."

"Like… 'Street poet's heroic stand against violence'?" The Chief read a headline out loud. The report was accompanied by a large photo of Sakakibara smiling on his hospital bed. "And you just happened to be there?"

"Yes. The incident happened while Detective Suzuki and I were tailing him."

"We have two problems." The Chief folded his arms. "The first concerns your actions. You're bound to be pilloried in the press for not having broken the fight up sooner."

"Yes, I'm ready for that. It's all my responsibility. Detective Suzuki wanted to go in right away, but I stopped him.

"Well, I guess we'll find a way round that one somehow. Which brings me to the other problem… have the papers got their facts right concerning the case?"

"More or less."

"Nevertheless, you believe Sakakibara murdered that bathhouse girl?"

"It can't be anyone else."

"However…" The Chief looked serious as he rose from his chair and walked slowly over to the window. It was as hot as ever, and Taguchi wiped the sweat from the back of his neck. He knew what the Chief was going to say.

The Chief turned to him, a puzzled look on his face. "I just don't get it. How can someone like this commit a murder? Was it all an act for your benefit?"

"I believe he helped that old man because he needed helping."

"It's not just that. According to your investigations, there's nothing to suggest he had any grudge against the victim, right?"

"There isn't—in fact, I'm sure he *didn't* have any grudge against her."

"So that just makes his motive for murder even weaker, doesn't it? So why do you think it is Sakakibara? What exactly is the basis for your conviction?"

"I can't explain it very well, but…" Taguchi searched for the right words to express what he wanted to say, but he could not find them. For want of a better way to put it, he said simply, "Sakakibara himself is telling me that he is the murderer." It wasn't exactly accurate, but in a sense it was what Taguchi believed.

"He's confessed?" The Chief's eyes popped.

"He hasn't actually confessed," responded Taguchi. "I know it sounds odd, but he's taunting me and deliberately challenging the police. It comes across like he's yelling that he killed her, that he's the murderer."

"I see." The Chief nodded slowly. It seemed from his expression that he had no idea what Taguchi was getting at. "But we can't arrest him on the basis of your conviction."

"I know that."

"And now Sakakibara's become the neighborhood hero. If you pursue him despite your lack of proof, you may well come under attack from the press."

"I'm also aware of that, but I just want a little more time." Taguchi looked the Chief directly in the face. It would be enough if he could discover the motive. If he could just do that, Sakakibara would probably give himself away without being pushed. "Please let me investigate him for a little longer."

The Chief sat in silence, his arms still folded. Taguchi took that to mean his tacit approval and, bowing his head briefly, he left the Chief's office.

Taguchi went to Peace Villa apartments to pay a visit to the hostess, Mineko. She was all dressed up on her way out to visit Sakakibara in hospital.

"Well, let me accompany you to the hospital," said Taguchi. Mineko scowled in irritation, but she seemed unable to refuse outright and set off without a word.

"There's something I've been wanting to ask you," he commented to her profile as he walked alongside her. In the bright sunlight, she looked even younger than when he had seen her in the dimly lit bar. Perhaps the victim, Kazuko Watanabe, would have looked this young if he'd seen her in the light of day too.

"Were Sakakibara and Kazuko sleeping together?"

Mineko shrugged. "None of us have that sort of relationship with Sensei."

"But you're men and women, right? It would be more natural for there to be a physical relationship."

"Sensei's a poet."

"But he's a man. Or perhaps he's lacking in that respect?"

"Don't be silly." Mineko stopped and glared at Taguchi with contempt in her eyes. "Sensei's a fine man. But we don't have a sexual relationship. And neither did Kazu."

"You girls into platonic love? Now that's a surprise."

"Well, you detectives are just plain dumb, aren't you?" Mineko turned away and started walking again.

Taguchi stood for a while watching Mineko as she stalked off. She was short, and he could tell at a glance that her clothes were cheap. In fact, she was the very picture of a trashy bargirl. The customers who came to that back alley bar were after women more than they were after booze, and she must have been with any number of them. That must be why she and the other girls longed for platonic relations. It was because they only ever met men who were blatantly after their body that they hankered after someone calling themselves a poet, like Sakakibara. If Sakakibara behaved like all the other men, they almost certainly would not call him Sensei with so much affection and respect.

Taguchi was satisfied with things thus far. But something was just not quite right. Neither Sakakibara or the girls seemed to realize it, but there was something fishy going on. He could not help feeling that the pleasantry was somewhat forced, the relationship fabricated. Perhaps the murder had been caused by the breakdown of that fabricated relationship?

Taguchi started walking again, but he lost the urge to catch up with Mineko. By the time he got to the hospital and went into Sakakibara's room, Mineko was arranging some flowers she had bought on the way in a vase. The air conditioning was not working and the room was quite hot. Nevertheless, Sakakibara looked cheerful and was sitting up in bed. When he saw Taguchi, he grinned.

"Am I under surveillance again today? You'll never solve the crime coming here."

"You seem pretty well."

"I am well. This hospital room is a lot more comfortable than my tiny home."

"I guess you've seen the papers."

"Sure. The nurse brought them for me."

"So how does it feel being the neighborhood hero?"

"It's not me at all," said Sakakibara with an abashed smile. It was clear from his face that he wasn't just being modest. He really was embarrassed, thought Taguchi. He had the feeling that this man's emotions were always awkward.

Sakakibara reached out a hand and picked up a cigarette off the table. Mineko quickly lit a match and held it out for him. Sakakibara looked self-conscious again.

"I asked the reporters not to make such a big thing out of it. It's really so embarrassing, I didn't even want it to be in the papers."

"How very self-effacing of you."

"Perhaps I'm shy."

"You're being unusually unassuming today, aren't you?" Taguchi looked at Sakakibara teasingly. Mineko glared at him.

"Sensei is a wonderful person."

"No, I'm not," Sakakibara blushed. "You girls really are living on the edge. Compared to you I'm utterly irresponsible."

"No, Sensei, you *are* a great person. Much more so than some petty detective."

Taguchi smiled wryly, saying nothing, but he recalled what he had been thinking on the way over here, matching it with the way the pair of them were talking now.

There was something strangely translucent about Sakakibara and Mineko's conversation.

He fully understood the feeling that Mineko and also the dead Kazuko had demanded something emotionally from Sakakibara. From their point of view, reality was sometimes fun but it was also tough and unhappy. So when a man calling himself a poet had come along making what for them seemed a fairytale world, it provided them with an escape from their harsh reality and they were making the most it. Young girls needed a prince, and Sakakibara probably fulfilled that role for them.

But why did Sakakibara need them?

If Sakakibara had been living off them like a pimp, then things would be clear. Even if they were merely linked by a sexual relationship, Taguchi would consider it natural. He had seen it so many times before—and if it had been that kind of relationship, there probably would have been no murder case now.

But Sakakibara had formed an unnatural relationship with the girls. From the girls' point of view it was natural, but for Sakakibara surely it was anything but?

To put it another way, for the girls, Sakakibara was a fairytale prince, but Sakakibara probably did not see himself that way.

Was it this gap in awareness between them that had led to the murder?

If so, then just how did Sakakibara perceive himself?

What was it that he'd said?

What had the line been? Something about woman as slave to the muse, and the poet as slave to woman. It was apparently something that Baudelaire had said, but Taguchi was interested in why Sakakibara had quoted it.

If he asked Sakakibara to his face, he would probably say, "I'm like a slave to those girls." But Sakakibara's exhibitionism bordered on the abnormal, carrying around that Baudelaire anthology, and putting up the sign "Contemporary Poetry Appreciation Society" on the door of his tiny apartment.

In which case he was probably subconsciously likening himself to the muse. And if so, wouldn't that mean the girls were his slaves?

During the time Sakakibara was in hospital, Taguchi met up with a number of people to find out more about him. Of interest were the accounts given by a fairly well-known poet by the name of Ko Fujimura, and a former college friend.

Ko Fujimura had never met Sakakibara, but had apparently read some of his poetry.

"I used to be involved with a publisher that holds the T. A. Poetry Award, which is a pretty authoritative prize. He used to enter it every time. But he was apparently never selected."

"Ah."

"I was on the panel of judges, and he once wrote demanding to know why his poem hadn't been selected. He wanted to know the reason. He sounded pretty full of himself, which is why the name Tetsuya Sakakibara has stuck in my memory."

"Sorry to be so crude, but were his poems any good?"

"They're very sensual, and in that respect I think some of them are quite good, it's just that they're somewhat saccharine. It's like there's no rigorousness in his view of reality, or perhaps it's that there's something lacking in the way he relates to the world."

"I think I know what you mean," laughed Taguchi. This was true, but he was more interested in how Sakakibara had kept entering the poetry competition, and had even written to the judges.

The old college friend's account backed up what Ko Fujimura had told him. At college, the words that Sakakibara had been fond of quoting were not by Baudelaire, but that famous line uttered by Byron, "I awoke one morning and found myself famous."

"That's why," the friend told Taguchi, "at that time I thought it would be Sakakibara, not Kyo Sasanuma, who would become a popular writer. He was precocious, a real go-getter. I'm amazed that it turned out the other way round."

These two statements were consistent in that Sakakibara's current lifestyle was somewhat removed from reality, but he himself longed for worldly fame. And his was an uncommonly intense longing for fame. However, that ambition had never been satisfied, not even once. His heart must be full of disappointment. Could it be that Kazuko and Mineko had been necessary to him in order to soothe his disenchantment?

Taguchi decided to talk to Mineko once more. Why had Sakakibara needed the girls, and what on earth did they mean to him? Things were still hazy, but he had the feeling he was beginning to understand. He wanted something concrete he could hold onto. If he could just clear these points up, he might possibly discover Sakakibara's motive for killing Kazuko Watanabe.

That evening, he headed for Julie's bar. There was no sign of Mineko, and when he commented to the manageress that it must be her day off, the answer came back, "Mine-chan won't be coming back at all."

"At all?"

"She quit."

"You're not telling me…" A thought had popped into Taguchi's mind that put a gleam in his eyes. "She's not getting married, is she?"

"How come you knew?"

"It's true, then?"

"Yes. An old boyfriend from her hometown she hadn't seen for several years turned up and asked her to marry him. She told me she was going back to Akita to get married."

"Getting married…" A slight shiver ran through Taguchi's chest.

Kazuko had been killed just before her wedding. Now Mineko was in the same situation as she had been in.

Will Sakakibara kill Mineko too?

Taguchi left Julie's and headed for Peace Villa apartments.

Mineko was in her room packing her bags.

When Taguchi told her, "I hear you're getting married," she wiped the sweat off her brow with the back of her hand and then grinned at him.

"Yeah, a guy from my hometown. He wants me despite everything."

"Sakakibara will be lonely, won't he? You'll no longer be around for him."

"I guess." There was a fleeting expression of triumph on Mineko's face.

"Have you told him you're getting married yet?"

"I'll go to the hospital tomorrow to tell him. I'm sure he'll be pleased for me. He always tells us he wants to see us happy. He often says it. Although I don't know if marriage is happiness really."

"How old are you?"

"Twenty-one."

"The same age as Kazuko then." Taguchi hesitated.

There was definitely a possibility that Mineko would be killed, in which case he should probably warn her not to inform Sakakibara of her marriage. But he stopped himself. Mineko would probably just laugh it off, and also he had a somewhat imprudent urge to make a "bet." He wanted to set a trap for Sakakibara, and this stopped him from saying anything. If he could trap Sakakibara—

"Detective, there's something I want to ask you."

Jogged out of his thoughts by Mineko's studied formality, Taguchi replied, "What's that?"

"Are the police allowed to rummage through anyone's apartment at will?"

"What are you talking about?"

"It's just when I started packing that I noticed, but I'm missing a makeup set. Did the police take it?"

"Why do you think it was the police?"

"If it had been a thief, he would have taken money. It must have been the police. But it's not that I'm asking for it back or anything."

"Sorry, but the police don't engage in that sort of petty thieving," Taguchi smiled wryly. But the next moment his smile disappeared and his expression hardened. "When did it go missing?"

"What?"

"I'm asking you when the makeup set disappeared."

"I don't know. And I've got loads of other makeup, so I don't need it back."

"What exactly was it that went missing?"

"Don't bother about it."

"Even if you don't mind, I do. I need to know. I want you to tell me exactly what it was that was taken."

"A makeup set. Cream, lipstick, eyebrow pencil, that sort of thing."

"I see."

"Do you know who took it?"

"I think I just might," replied Taguchi vaguely, his eyes narrowed.

The next evening it started raining.

With each passing car, sheaves of rain shone white in the headlights. It showed no sign of easing up. In his sheltered location on watch, Detective Suzuki stirred slightly and looked at Taguchi.

"Will Sakakibara go out in this?"

"Probably," responded Taguchi, his gaze fixed on the hospital. "At least, Mineko came this afternoon and told him she's getting married. And what's more, Sakakibara can walk again."

"What was Sakakibara's motive for killing Kazuko Watanabe? You know it, don't you, boss?"

"I'm not certain I'm right, though." Taguchi lit a cigarette, never taking his eyes from the hospital. He thought he knew what it was, but if he was wrong then Sakakibara was unlikely to leave the hospital. "I just tried to imagine what sort of person he is."

Taguchi spoke slowly, as if reconfirming his own thoughts to himself. "He doesn't have a proper job, he lives in a tiny, cheap apartment, and he spends what little money he makes selling mimeographed collections of his poetry on drinking in a back alley bar. The girls who work in the bar and the bathhouse all call him Sensei. This is the Sakakibara you see on the surface."

"So carefree! Sounds pretty enviable to me."

"I also thought that to begin with, too." Taguchi smiled sardonically. Nobody had come out of the hospital yet, and the light was still on in Sakakibara's room. "But looking at it rationally, Sakakibara's lifestyle is fake, it has no substance. When we were watching him, he hardly sold any of his poetry, did he? Can he really live on that? Let alone go drinking in bars. The fact he's been able to do that is because those girls have been helping him. Or to put it simply, he's pretty much like a pimp. However much he calls it a poetic relationship, I think he's just using words and airs to cover up for the lack of substance in his life. That pompous sign "Contemporary Poetry Appreciation Society," carrying around that Baudelaire volume, and even the girls—they're all nothing more than decorative means to cover up his empty life."

"It really sounds like a house of cards, doesn't it?"

"House of cards?" Smiling, Taguchi flicked away his cigarette butt. "I guess it is. He's far more desperate for fame than most people, but he hasn't achieved it. In other words, he's a failure. You could say he's become the lord of his own house of cards in order to escape that sense of humiliation. Therefore, it wasn't because he liked the girls that he kept them close to hand. They were just cards that he used to build his house. They were objects that he could commiserate with."

"So when one of them decided to marry, it meant the loss of one of the cards."

"It's not just that he lost one of the cards, but that someone who should have been oppressed by a miserable existence transformed into someone happier than him. It must have been intolerable for Sakakibara. He was probably gripped with the fear that his house of cards would come tumbling down. So he killed her."

"But he must have known that even if he killed her, he would never return to where he was before."

"No. I think he believed that if he killed Kazuko, she would once again be a pitiable woman. You remember that despite her heavy makeup, she had just slipped her feet into sandals?"

"Yes, I remember. It really stood out as being oddly mismatched."

"That makeup was applied by Sakakibara after he killed her. He used makeup that he stole from Mineko's room."

"Why would he do such a thing?"

"She had become a happy twenty-one-year-old girl about to be married, and he wanted to return her to being a bathhouse girl, I think. I can't think of any other reason."

Taguchi lit up another cigarette. Rain was still falling. The hospital was enveloped in deep silence.

"There is one thing I just don't understand," said Suzuki in a low voice. "If that's the sort of guy he is, why would he get himself hurt rescuing a child or saving an old guy from a beating? It takes a pretty terrific sort of guy to do that sort of thing."

"It is terrific. But doesn't it strike you as a bit abnormal?"

"Abnormal?"

"Sakakibara even got into a fight with some yakuza thug to help out Kazuko Watanabe. That's terrific. But a normal person wouldn't do something like that with no regard for the danger to themselves, would they? Let alone three times. It's got nothing to do with courage. It's just that most people would naturally think of their life, their family, or their lover or whatever and hesitate. It's more natural to remain an onlooker. Yet Sakakibara flew to the rescue not just once, but a full three times. There was nothing in his life to make him hesitate. The only thing holding him back was fear, but his sense of duty wouldn't allow him to give in to this. It'd be too shameful. He's a bit out of synch with most people. He isn't so much terrific, as abnormal, I'd say. And I think the flip side of that is that he's capable of killing someone."

Taguchi peered at his wristwatch in the dim light. It was nearly midnight.

"Does he know we're watching him?" Suzuki was beginning to get impatient.

"Most likely," nodded Taguchi. "It probably will occur to him that we're tailing him. It'd be strange if it didn't."

"He'll come out even so?"

"I'd bet on him coming out, myself. If I were him, that's what I'd do. Once it's occurred to him that there's something he has to do, he'll be a slave to that sense of duty of his. That's just the way he is. He's already killed Kazuko Watanabe—because he thought that if he didn't, his house of cards would come tumbling down. Now, if he doesn't kill Mineko, then he will have to admit that that the first murder was a mistake. I can't believe he'd do that. Sakakibara's biggest fear is not that the police will get him, but that his house of cards will collapse. If that happens, then he'll be nothing more than a hangover from a squalid life. He wouldn't be able to live with that. So he'll come out."

It was past midnight, getting on for two in the morning when Suzuki suddenly whispered, "Ah! That's him. Sakakibara's on the move."

Getting soaked in the rain, Sakakibara walked slowly past the two detectives. Seen from behind, with his shoulders drooping and dragging his left leg, he had nothing of the arrogant murderer about him. As Taguchi followed him, he felt a bleakness emanating from him.

Sakakibara never turned round once.

He stopped before Peace Villa apartments. The lights were out in all of the rooms, and it was wrapped in silence.

For some time, Sakakibara stared up at the second floor. Then he shrugged slightly, and went in. Taguchi and Suzuki followed him.

Everything that happened after that was just as Taguchi had imagined.

There was a woman's scream. Taguchi and Suzuki burst into Mineko's room just as Sakakibara had twisted a hand towel around her neck.

Suzuki sent Sakakibara's skinny body flying and held him down. Sakakibara offered little resistance. He watched his own hands being handcuffed, and then looked at Taguchi.

"I knew you were following me. This way, you'll be able to get a good night's sleep."

"You too," responded Taguchi, his voice gruff.

The Detective

The call came on March third, the day of the Doll's Festival. With hindsight, this date—a festival dedicated to children—was indeed significant.

It had been a cold day. Incredibly, after the recent run of warm spring days, light, fluffy snow started falling in the morning and showed no sign of let-up by nightfall. Fifteen centimeters had settled even in the heart of the metropolis.

Akasaka police station was at the hub of a thriving entertainment district, thronged with round-the-clock hostess bars and high-class Japanese restaurants that came to life after sundown. That night, however, the traffic was subdued and the neon lights lacked their usual brilliance.

Detective Ono, gazing out of the window at the falling snowflakes, pictured his daughter, now age six, playing excitedly before the gorgeous display of traditional dolls set up in the living room. He turned to his colleague to talk about it, but Detective Tasaka was busy at his desk writing up the day's report.

Tasaka had transferred from the Ueno police station two years earlier, and Ono had heard he had divorced his wife before the move. However, that was all Ono knew, since whenever the subject came up, Tasaka's expression hardened and he lapsed into silence as if he were still suffering from an open wound.

Did Tasaka and his wife have any kids? wondered Ono. Perhaps it was because of the date that his mind had turned to such matters. He was just thinking he would ask Tasaka about it sometime while they were out drinking, when the telephone rang.

Ono reached out a hand to pick up the receiver.

"Is that the police?" he heard a woman's voice inquire. It was a firm voice, belonging to a woman of indeterminate age. When he replied in the affirmative, there was a pause before she said, "Please come over right away. My son has committed suicide."

"Suicide?" echoed Ono, thinking her voice was remarkably calm for someone whose child had just died. She spoke in a steady, flat tone, as if talking about something that did not concern her.

"May I have your name?"

"Igarashi. It's the house behind the fire station. Please come right away." Having said this, the woman hung up. She had twice requested that they come right away, but somehow he felt no sense of urgency in her voice. How could she sound so indifferent? Perhaps she was the no-nonsense type of mother—or perhaps she was in a daze. Ono really could not tell which.

"A suicide?" asked Tasaka across from him

"So it seems," nodded Ono. "A woman by the name of Igarashi said her son had—" Suddenly he realized he had heard the name before. "She said she lived behind the fire station. The actress Kyoko Igarashi lives somewhere around there, doesn't she? Perhaps it's her."

"The actress?" Tasaka's face twisted in a grimace. Taken aback, Ono was just about to ask Tasaka whether he had anything against actresses, when he grinned. "If it's Kyoko Igarashi, then we'll have the chance of seeing her at close quarters. Can't be bad, huh?"

It was unlike Tasaka to say something like that. He was utterly serious, and rarely joked about a case. There was also something particularly unnatural about this joke.

Strange, thought Ono, but he said nothing as the two of them headed out.

It was still snowing. Ono raised the collar of his raincoat and, screwing up his face against the snowflakes, looked up at the night sky.

"Surely it can't really be Kyoko Igarashi the actress, though."

"Why's that?"

"She said it was her son that had killed himself."

"So?"

"She's better known for the size of her bust and her scandalous lifestyle than for her acting. She can't be any older than twenty-five or twenty-six—which would make her son about five or six at most. There's no way a child of that age could commit suicide."

Ono thought of his own six-year-old daughter. The idea that she would commit suicide was ludicrous.

Tasaka glanced briefly up at the night sky before murmuring, "I guess not." His voice struck Ono as diaphanous. This man did not have kids, he thought, and was probably not the slightest bit interested in them.

They could tell which house it was right away. It was not large, but it was stylish and looked as though it had cost a good deal of money. It was styled after a Western medieval castle, cutting a pretty picture amidst the snowy landscape.

Ono pressed the bell, and they waited two or three minutes before a thin girl of about seventeen or eighteen stuck her head out. In the light of the entrance porch, they could see her face was very pale and fearful. When they showed their police badges, she said hoarsely, "Sensei is inside."

"By Sensei, do you mean the actress Kyoko Igarashi?" queried Ono. The girl nodded silently, but she looked suspicious. She probably assumed they knew very well who this house belonged to.

A flicker of puzzlement ran over Ono's face. What on earth was the age of the child who had killed himself? He glanced at Tasaka, but he did not look in the slightest perplexed. The two of them brushed the snow off their coats in the porch before following the maid in. Ono caught Tasaka muttering under his breath, his voice thick with scorn, "The scandal actress, huh?" He worried that the maid might have heard, but her retreating figure did not reveal anything amiss.

Kyoko Igarashi was reclining on a sofa in the living room. Upon seeing the two detectives she rose sluggishly to her feet, bowed her head, and said, "Thank you for coming."

She really was beautiful, with the sharp outlines of a modern beauty. But something deep within Tasaka refused to acknowledge her looks. Subconsciously, his eyes were picking out all of her faults. Her mouth was too big, as were her eyes. More than anything, this woman lacked the purity of youth. He could almost smell the whiff of decadence she exuded. And those dark circles under her eyes were surely not from the shock of losing her son, but the result of her habitual wild lifestyle.

Tasaka knew that he should not prejudge Kyoko Igarashi, yet he could not help being aware of the fact that, not only was she an actress, but one who was famous for her immoral behavior. And as long he was unable to come to terms with certain painful memories, he was unlikely to change his view of her.

The door opened and a middle-aged man came in. He introduced himself as a doctor from a nearby hospital. "I came as soon as I received the call, but I was too late," he said matter-of-factly.

Tasaka and Ono were taken upstairs to the child's bedroom. What first struck them on entering the room was not the boy's dead body, but the sheer number of plastic models crowded in it, covering the shelves and the desk, and hanging from the ceiling. It felt like the entire room was buried in models. Strangely they were all of aircraft, nothing else. This kid must have really liked airplanes.

The boy was lying on the bed by the window, his face covered with a white cloth.

Expressionless, Tasaka lifted the cloth to reveal the face of a child of about five or six, frozen in a rictus of agony.

"The cause of death was poison. According to the mother, he ate pellets of rat poison provided by the public health authority," explained the doctor calmly.

As he listened, Tasaka's thoughts were elsewhere. He was recalling the dead body of an even smaller child, one who had died an even more pitiful death than this—his two-year-old daughter, her tiny body curled up in a fetal position, her limbs rigid in the muddy water. Inevitably, he vividly recalled her agonized face as he looked at the one before him now.

Tasaka turned to Kyoko Igarashi, his face ashen.

She was crouched in the doorway, gazing with unfocused eyes at one of the models hanging from the ceiling.

"Why do you think it was suicide?"

Her shoulders quivering, Kyoko turned her gaze to Tasaka. "The boy killed himself."

"I'm asking you why—the reason you think it was suicide."

His tone had hardened, as if interrogating her, so Ono tried to soften it by changing the form of the question. "Your son must be about five or six years old, right?"

"He's six." Her gaze swam over to the bed.

Ono calmly continued, "It's hard to imagine a child of that age committing suicide, isn't it? He might have eaten the poison pellets by mistake."

"No," she replied, shaking her head. "He knew he shouldn't eat them."

"And so you decided it was suicide?" Tasaka spoke harshly, irritated at Ono's gentle questioning. Kyoko muttered something in a low voice. Unable to catch it, he said loudly, "Speak up a bit!" He could feel the apprehensiveness in Ono standing next to him, but he just could not control his own emotions. Ono probably had no idea how he was feeling, but then he had no desire to be understood.

Kyoko looked blankly at Tasaka. "He wrote a suicide note. That's why—"

"A suicide note?"

Ono and Tasaka exchanged a glance. A suicide note written by a six-year-old? Did such a thing ever exist? Was it possible?

Without a word she left the room and came back with a piece of paper.

On it was a picture of an airplane drawn in pastel crayons, a jetliner by the looks of it. "Daddy's jet" was written underneath. It looked like a pretty typical drawing by a six-year-old boy, nothing more.

"This is the suicide note?" asked Tasaka, frowning.

"Turn it over," replied Kyoko in a low voice.

On the back there were a few words written in blue crayon. "I'm going to join Daddy."

Unsure immediately of how to interpret these few words, Tasaka and Ono looked at each other. "What does it mean?"

Kyoko's large eyes filled with tears. Words suddenly started pouring out of her as though a dam had burst inside her. "My son has gone to join my husband. When I got home from work, he was already dead. And this was next to him. It's a suicide note he left to me. My husband was a pilot, but he died in a plane crash last year. When my boy asked me where he was, I told him he was in heaven. And so he must have believed that if he died he would go to heaven where his father was. And then he—those poison pellets, I'd warned him that he would die if he ate them…"

Kyoko burst into violent weeping. The pilot father who had died in a crash; the young mother who had told their child the father was in heaven; and the six-year-old son—all the ingredients for her tears were so conveniently in place, thought Tasaka.

The more she talked, the more Tasaka was convinced she was lying. He watched her coldly as she wept. This was probably a performance to hide something. An actress was an actress regardless of what she was best known for. Putting on a performance to move witless detectives to tears was no doubt child's play for her.

Tasaka realized he was being overly strict with her. But deep in his heart he felt an antagonism that he was powerless to remedy. It made him feel bleak and sluggish inside.

Unaware of the cold, dark emotions Tasaka was experiencing, the good-natured Ono appeared to thoroughly sympathize with the unfortunate actress, and started asking her for more details.

According to Kyoko, she had been involved in diverse scandals with various men, but her one true love had been the pilot who died in a plane crash the year before.

"Today was my boy's sixth birthday," she told Ono, biting her lip, "so I knocked off work earlier than usual and came home, but…" Again she bowed her head and sobbed.

Blinking, Ono looked away. Tasaka, however, was apparently unimpressed by such melodrama and his expression grew even harder.

A woman like that doesn't even know the meaning of true love, he thought. She probably did not even feel a mother's affection for her child. These were just crocodile tears.

For the time being, Tasaka and Ono decided to take the "suicide note" with them back to the police station.

It was still snowing when they left.

"I'm fed up with this weather," shrugged Ono, glancing up at the night sky. Then he lightly patted his coat pocket. "You know,

I'm not at all convinced about this suicide note. I mean, really, a six-year-old boy writes a suicide note before killing himself? What do you think?"

"Of course it isn't suicide!" declared Tasaka. He was certain of this, although less as a result of the interview with Kyoko Igarashi than from his own conviction.

"You think so too?" Ono smiled happily. "Of course it was an accident, right?"

"Wrong," said Tasaka as if vomiting up something vile from the depths of his soul. He glared into the dark snowy night. "It was murder. That woman killed her son."

"Murder?" Ono's eyes widened. The thought had apparently never even occurred to him. "Why do you think that?"

"That kind of woman is certainly capable of killing her own child," said Tasaka. He knew it sounded outrageous, but he could think of no other way to put it. He could not bring himself to tell Ono that he was speaking from his own experience.

Ono was baffled. "What a shocking thing to say! I would never have thought you knew anything about actresses."

"I don't. But with that sort of woman—well, you can just tell."

"Why?" It was unusual for the mild-mannered Ono to be so insistent, so he must have been really taken aback by Tasaka's comments.

"No reason. But it's murder, I'm telling you. That woman killed her six-year-old child," said Tasaka firmly.

Back at the station, the Chief looked somewhat bemused by their report.

"It seems you have quite different views," he commented, stretching back in his chair. The wooden swivel chair groaned under the weight of his considerable bulk. "First, let's hear what you have to say, Ono."

"Whichever way you look at it, it must have been an accident," he told the Chief, then glanced over at Tasaka as if to check his reaction. Tasaka was gazing out of the window. Looking back at the Chief, Ono continued, "I think the child had probably forgotten his mother's warning when he ate the rat poison. It often happens with children of that age. In fact, just a few days ago there was a case of a five-year-old girl who died after eating rat poison even though her mother had warned her not to. It must have been in the papers."

"Ah yes, I read about that," nodded the Chief, lighting up a cigarette. The cigarette looked disturbingly thin against his enormous hand. "But then, if it was an accident, what do you make of this suicide note?" He lightly tapped the child's drawing on the desk before him with the tip of his finger.

Glancing at the crayon drawing of an airplane, Ono answered, "There are various possibilities, but I don't think it is a suicide note."

"But the meaning is clear from what's written here, 'I'm going to join Daddy,' isn't it?"

"Yes, you can take it that way, but I think it's more likely to be an explanation of the picture. If you look closely there are only two people in the plane, no doubt the boy and his father. Therefore he probably just wanted to explain that the drawing was about his desire to go flying in an airplane together with his father. At six years old, there isn't such a clear distinction between reality and imagination. I really don't think it's all that strange for the boy to have had the feeling he and his dead father were in a plane together."

"So his mother—Kyoko Igarashi—is mistaken?"

"I think so, yes. Any mother would be upset at coming home from work to find their child dead. Even more so, given that today was the boy's birthday. In her agitated state, I don't think it's unreasonable for her to have taken it for her child's suicide note."

"And what do you think?" the Chief turned to look at Tasaka. The chair beneath him creaked again. Ono also looked at Tasaka.

"I'm afraid I disagree," said Tasaka, looking squarely into the Chief's eyes. "From what I saw, that woman was not in an agitated state, and she wasn't even upset. She was quite composed. I can only think that she was putting on a skillful performance of the role of a pitiful mother who had just lost her son. In order to cover up for murder—"

"It struck you as a performance?" Ono stared at Tasaka, shocked.

"Yes," said Tasaka simply. "Did you think she was really weeping?"

"Those were real tears!"

"No, she isn't that sincere."

"You seem to have a peculiar prejudice, that because she's an actress anything she does is a performance," retorted Ono.

"Hang on," said the Chief with an ironic smile. "In any case, let's hear Tasaka out. So you think it's murder?"

"Yes, I do."

"But he was her own son, wasn't he? And he was only six. Kids are at their most adorable at that age. Could she really have killed him?"

"There are people who don't adore their children, you know." Tasaka stopped speaking and looked out of the window. To Ono, his profile looked terribly cold. True, Tasaka was usually exceptionally serious, and could even be stubborn and inflexible, but Ono had never once considered him heartless. Today, however, there was something abnormal about him. His behavior even seemed unreasonably cruel.

The Chief contemplated Tasaka with a rather puzzled look. "So you're saying Kyoko Igarashi is that sort of mother?"

"Yes. She's that type, yes."

"You're awfully confident about this, aren't you? But if it was murder as you're saying, why did she deliberately attract suspicion by saying the child had committed suicide? Don't you think that's odd? The safest thing would have been to burn this picture and claim the child had eaten the poison by mistake, wouldn't it?"

"Yes, that's true. However, Kyoko Igarashi is no ordinary woman. She's an actress."

"What has that got to do with it?"

"What matters most is her popularity. It probably would have been safest to claim it was an accident, but then she would have come under fire as a mother for not having paid enough attention. If the mass media wrote something like that about her, it would have been fatal to her career. However, if it transpired that the six-year-old boy had been so attached to his dead father that he committed suicide, then it would be just the sort of melodrama that people love to follow. And if she was convincing in her portrayal of a grieving mother who had just lost her only son, far from being criticized she would become the darling of the mass media in one fell swoop."

"Are you really suggesting that Kyoko Igarashi went to such lengths to work everything out in order to kill her child?"

"A woman like that is certainly capable of it. Even this thing she claims to be a suicide note, we don't know when it was written. I think it was written at least a few days ago, but she just chose to use it today. Let me investigate this case. I'll strip away the disguise and reveal her true nature. Her dead child at least deserves that much."

The Chief did not respond right away. After thinking a moment, he told Tasaka, "There is something I'd like to ask you." His tone was rather formal. "Why are you so sure that it is murder? Common sense tells me it must be an accident, like Ono here says."

"It's murder. I'm absolutely convinced."

"It sounds to me as though perhaps you're a bit biased."

"Biased?" Ono noticed Tasaka blanch slightly.

"That's right," nodded the Chief. "You haven't got a grudge against Kyoko Igarashi that might have led you to believe she's a murderer, have you? Of course, I don't suppose you have, but I have to ask just in case."

"Of course I haven't." Tasaka was still pale.

"That's okay then." The Chief smiled. "In that case, I'll ask you to investigate."

"I'll definitely find proof of the crime," said Tasaka, the excitement showing on his face.

Ono was on his way out of the Chief's office with Tasaka when the Chief called him back. "Have you got a minute?" the Chief inquired, as if he had remembered something.

Even though Tasaka had gone, the Chief did not say anything straight away, but sat for a while, his chin resting on his hands, thinking. After a while, he raised his face and, looking somewhat hesitant, asked Ono, "What do you think?"

"You mean about the case? In my opinion—"

"No. I'm talking about Detective Tasaka. Has he got a grudge against Igarashi, do you think?"

"Are you asking my honest opinion?"

"Naturally."

"I don't know if he's got a grudge or not. All I can say is that he's been a bit abnormal today. He's usually a bit more cautious about judging a murder case."

"What is it about this case that is making him behave abnormally?"

"I don't know."

"I need to know." The Chief's chair creaked unpleasantly, as if reflecting his unease. "And I want you to find out," he continued. "If Detective Tasaka thinks this case is murder due to some preconception of his, then he needs to be stopped—for the sake of the police as well as his own sake, too."

"Understood."

"I'm sure I don't need to stress to you that I'm not telling you to follow Detective Tasaka's every move. I want you to work alongside him and to assist him. If things go wrong, he'll be meat for the media."

Having said all of this, the smile returned to the corners of the Chief's mouth. There was another loud groan from his chair, and he commented, "This chair's really seen better days, hasn't it?

The next morning, the case was all over the newspapers, much as Tasaka had predicted. All the headlines used virtually the same wording, clearly showing how the media were treating the story. A typical example was, "Boy of six commits suicide? Actress Kyoko Igarashi's only son dies."

The question mark indicated the doubt as to whether a six-year-old child really could commit suicide, while the fact that they expressly mentioned her by name indicated the status of the story as celebrity gossip.

Tasaka was in the office reading the reports in the papers.

Of course, there was nothing in any of the papers to suggest the possibility of murder. And almost all had included a photo of Kyoko beside herself with grief. The overall tone was one of melodrama. This was also just as Tasaka had predicted. The mass media was fêting her as a tragic heroine.

Tasaka threw down a paper and looked out of the window. The snow that had been falling steadily all day and night had at last stopped, and the morning sun shining through the window was dazzling.

He rose to his feet saying he would pay a visit on Kyoko Igarashi, while Ono warned him, "Don't overdo things." Tasaka was well aware of Ono's concern that he might be too heavy-handed, but he merely replied, "I won't," and left.

It was almost ten o'clock. He had expected there to be a media scrum around Kyoko Igarashi's house, yet when he arrived there was no sign of it.

He rang the bell and the same young maid as before stuck her head out to say that the actress was not at home.

"NTV sent a car around to take Sensei to the studio," she told him. That would explain the absence of any media around the house, but he was outraged that Kyoko could calmly carry on with her television work the day after the death of her only son. It merely convinced him even more that yesterday's tears had been all show.

That's one to me, Tasaka told himself.

"Did she really warn her son not to eat those rat poison pellets?" he asked the maid.

"Why would you ask such a thing?" she retorted with studied formality, her face rigid. She had probably been cautioned by Kyoko Igarashi to watch what she said.

"I'm just asking. So?"

"Sensei loved her son very much."

"That's not an answer. I asked about the rat poison."

"There's no reason she wouldn't have warned him."

"But you did not actually witness her do so?"

"But—"

"That's all I wanted to know." Tasaka turned on his heel and walked off, ignoring the maid's protests.

He arrived at the NTV studios in Kojimachi to find Kyoko Igarashi busy with a drama series due to start in the middle of the following month.

He decided to wait for her outside studio number two where the "On Air" sign was lit up. A group of showbiz reporters was sitting nearby, also evidently waiting for her. Feigning indifference Tasaka listened in on their gossip.

"She's done pretty well out of her kid's death, hasn't she?"

"It sure landed her the lead role in this TV drama."

"I heard it was all set to go to Fujiko Arakawa."

"Yeah. The thing is that her acting is great, but she's not all that well known and that worried the TV station bosses."

"And then this goes and happens. A widow loses her only son— it's exactly what the drama series is about, isn't it? If it's covered in all the big papers, it'll be full marks on the promotion front."

"Then I heard the director called her up late last night."

"What I heard was that he actually drove over to her place in heavy snow and begged her to take it."

"I'll bet she jumped at it."

"Of course she did. This drama will likely be broadcast during the Sunday golden hour. If the audience ratings are good, she'll be an overnight star."

"But she's just lost her only son! Wasn't she a bit reluctant to start work on the drama the very next day?"

"That's an ordinary person's way of thinking. Celebrities are a different breed—even if their old man was kicked to death, they'd find a way to benefit from the situation. And she had money problems, too."

"She was short of money?"

"Pretty bad, from what I heard. You don't make much money from scandals."

They all burst into gales of laughter. Just then, the "On Air" sign went out. They all got up en masse, opened the heavy door to the studio and went in.

Tasaka did not immediately follow them, but sat for a while replaying their conversation in his mind.

To some extent, lies were part and parcel of showbiz reporting, but it was unlikely that all of what they said was just irresponsible talk; they were generally alert to people's secrets. Even the rumor about Kyoko Igarashi being in financial difficulty probably had some basis in fact. If so, it might well have some bearing on this case.

Having thought this much, Tasaka got to his feet and went into the studio.

In the studio they were holding a press conference for the cast, who were still in full costume. At the center of it all, dressed in a subdued kimono, sat Kyoko Igarashi amidst a shower of camera flashes.

Tasaka stood at a distance from the crowd and for a while observed her being interviewed.

The interview appeared to be drawing to a close. She had tended to look down while answering questions, but now, raising her eyes she caught sight of Tasaka. A momentary expression of confusion mixed with panic crossed her face. The reporters also apparently noticed it, for a number of faces turned in Tasaka's direction following her gaze.

As if to put them off, Tasaka approached and told them, stony faced, "I'm from the police. If you've finished your interview, I'd like to ask a few questions of my own."

"So what are the police investigating?" The reporters surrounded Tasaka, undisguised curiosity showing on their faces.

"It has nothing to do with you lot," Tasaka said sharply to keep them away.

Kyoko Igarashi glared furiously at Tasaka. "Come over here," she said, dragging him to a corner of the studio.

The reporters refrained from following, but they huddled together and watched intently from a distance.

"Why did you come barging in here?" demanded Kyoko, her face pale. "My life depends on this job. If any weird rumors start, it'll ruin everything."

"I went to your home but was told you were at work, so I had no choice but to come here. It never occurred to me you'd be working the day after your only son's death," said Tasaka with heavy irony.

"Are you being sarcastic?" asked Kyoko, her eyes stern.

"I'm only stating the obvious. But then it seems that common sense doesn't work in your world, does it?"

"I'm an actress. However sad I'm feeling, I have to work, if only for all my fans. I'm different from ordinary people."

"I heard you got the job on this drama thanks to your son's death." Tasaka knew he was being nasty.

"Are you saying I should have turned it down?" Kyoko's voice became shrill.

"No," answered Tasaka curtly, his face as calm as ever. "I'm impressed that you are capable of putting in a good performance. Most would be utterly incapable of doing so. By the way, did you really warn your son not to eat the rat poison?"

"Of course I did. I'm his mother!"

"Have you any proof?"

"Proof?" Her face crumpled. Her slender fingers clutching the sleeve of her kimono trembled. "Are you saying that I'm to blame for my son's death?"

"As a police officer, I just want to know the facts."

"I warned my son. Now please leave!"

"The proof?"

"I've got proof!"

"Your maid didn't know about it."

"There's the worker from the Public Health Office who brought the poison. My son came back from preschool just after he arrived and he warned him about it. Ask him—he'll confirm it. Unfortunately for you, I suppose."

Tasaka deliberately ignored the gibe, commenting "I guess I'd better go and ask at the health office, then."

Kyoko stamped her feet impatiently. "If you're quite finished, then can I ask you to leave? I have to go over to STV now."

"You're in hot demand, aren't you?"

"Anything wrong with that?"

"No, well, I'll just ask one more thing before I clear off. Is it true that you're having financial problems?"

"Whoever told you such a thing?" The color drained from Kyoko's face. Tasaka grinned. It seemed it was true. He had found a weak point of hers, although he did not yet know how to connect it to the crime.

"I just heard a rumor."

At that moment, a young girl who looked like a fledgling actress called over, "Igarashi Sensei!"

Kyoko glanced over at her and then said dryly, "That was all, then?" Without waiting for an answer, she walked quickly out of the studio.

Igarashi Sensei, is it? Tasaka watched her go with a wry smile. If it transpired that she had indeed killed her six-year-old son, then nobody would be calling her Sensei much longer.

A visitor had arrived for Detective Tasaka, so Ono went to reception to meet him in his place.

The man was about forty, and wore a moustache. After glancing sharply at Ono through his thick glasses, he said, "I have come on behalf of Kyoko Igarashi." He proffered his business card, upon which was written "Ichiro Yoshimuta, Director, ABC Productions."

Already? thought Ono, bracing himself.

"Excuse me, but are you Detective Tasaka?" asked Ichiro Yoshimuta.

"No," replied Ono. "He's out on an investigation at the moment. I'm his colleague, Detective Ono."

"Well, please tell him when he returns to stop harassing her."

"Harassing?" Ono's expression wavered.

Yoshimuta continued unperturbed, "It's clearly suicide, yet the police are still sniffing around as if there was something more to it. Look, show business is all about popularity ratings, so it's causing us a lot of bother."

"We don't know that it's suicide, you know," said Ono.

"It *is* suicide. There was even a suicide note, wasn't there? Didn't you see it yourself?" pressed Yoshimuta.

"Yes, I saw it," replied Ono. "But there remains some doubt as to whether a six-year-old child is capable of committing suicide. So we are investigating, just in case."

"But Detective Tasaka's method of investigating seems to be to interrogate Kyoko Igarashi as if she herself had killed her own child."

"Surely not."

"It's true—just now she came to me in floods of tears to tell me about it. Detective Tasaka came barging in on her while she was at work at a TV station and started treating her like a criminal right under the noses of a bunch of reporters there. This is absolutely going too far."

Shit, thought Ono. He really was overdoing it. This was not officially a murder case, and there was not even an incident room set up for it. In other words, it was an under-the-table investigation. They should be treading warily, yet here was Tasaka aggressively confronting the woman head on.

Apparently emboldened by Ono's silence, Yoshimuta continued, "Show business is precarious, and if any weird rumors got around it could be fatal. I really must ask you to consider this. If anything like this happens again, we will have no choice but to defend ourselves and take legal action against Detective Tasaka. Please tell him that," he added threateningly.

When Yoshimuta had left, Ono went to report to the Chief and said, "I would like to pay a visit to Ueno police station."

With arms folded, the Chief considered this and then queried, "You mean, to find out about Detective Tasaka?"

"Yes. I happen to have a friend from my police academy days stationed there; he's bound to know something. Tasaka's behavior on this case is really unlike him. If he carries on like this, things are bound to end badly. I'm concerned about him. If I can just find out why he's behaving like he is, I think I'll be able to help him."

"You're probably right. Okay, you'd better get going," replied the Chief.

Ono made his way through the slush-filled streets to Ueno with a heavy heart. He was about to inquire into Tasaka's secrets. Even if he was doing it for a good reason, to help Tasaka, there was nothing pleasant about it.

His old friend Detective Yokoi looked pleased to see Ono as he came out to greet him. It had been four years. After catching up with each other's latest news, Ono said casually, "I'm partnered with Detective Tasaka these days. He was here before, wasn't he?"

"Tasaka?" repeated Yokoi. "Ah, right, Detective Tasaka." He smiled. "He's extremely trustworthy, isn't he? A very serious man."

"Yes. But there's something that's worrying me."

"What's that?"

"How come he's still single? He's already thirty, after all."

"Why? Have you got a bride in mind for him?"

"Well, you know…" said Ono evasively. "I heard that he was married before, but is that true?"

"It's true. But they didn't get along. In the end they split up—even though they had a child."

"A child?" Ono was surprised. Given Tasaka's behavior during this case, he had assumed that he did not have any children of his own.

"She was a really cute little girl." A shadow passed over Yokoi's face.

"Did she die?"

"Yes. It was a horrible death, too. Tasaka's never been the same since."

"How did she die?"

"His wife was a bit flashy. After their daughter was born, she had an affair with a TV celebrity. And she went running after him, leaving the kid behind. She'd always wanted to be in showbiz, or something. The day she left, Detective Tasaka was busy with a murder investigation. The little girl—she was two and a half at the time—apparently tried to follow her mother, but fell down a drain. She couldn't get out again, and she died down there."

"Did she know her daughter had died?"

"Probably not," Yokoi continued, "And don't say anything of what I've told you to Detective Tasaka."

"Don't worry, I won't," responded Ono.

Ono felt he now understood why Tasaka was so abnormally interested in the current case, and why he was so quick to judge it as murder. Deep in his heart, this case must be superimposed on his own daughter's death and his wife's betrayal. But the knowledge did not lighten Ono's heart at all— in fact it made it heavier.

The official at the Public Health Office could not recall whether he had warned Kyoko Igarashi's son about the rat poison or not. His evasiveness emboldened Tasaka further. It seemed increasingly possible that it was murder.

By the time he left the Public Health Office, the sun was high in the sky and the snow was quickly melting. This morning the landscape had been pure white, but now it was converted into grubby slush.

Bit like Kyoko Igarashi, Tasaka told himself repeatedly as he headed for the kindergarten attended by Kyoko's son. She might be beautiful on the surface, but inside she was full of filth. So much so that she had sacrificed her own child without a qualm. Just like Misako, the wife that had abandoned Tasaka.

A "Closed" sign hung outside the kindergarten, no doubt due to the snow, but the headmistress and a teacher were there so he was able to ask about the dead child.

"It seems he was very attached to his deceased father," commented Tasaka.

"Oh yes," nodded the teacher. "Whenever we do drawing, he always does a picture of an airplane, and then explains that it's Daddy's jetliner. He really loved his father."

"What about his mother?"

"You mean Kyoko Igarashi?"

"Yes. Did he ever draw pictures of his mother?"

"If he was told to draw one, yes."

"Only then?"

"Yes."

"Isn't it usual for small children to draw pictures of their mothers?"

"Yes, well…" Suddenly the teacher became vague, apparently worried that Tasaka might infer something from what she said.

"What did you think when you heard about the suicide?"

She seemed relieved at the change of subject. "I was shocked!"

"Just that? Didn't you think it was odd? Weren't you a little doubtful as to whether a six-year-old child would commit suicide?" The teacher clammed up at Tasaka's barrage of questions. He turned to the middle-aged headmistress. "What do you think?" he queried. "Is there any record of a six-year-old child having committed suicide?"

"In this country, the youngest recorded suicide was actually seven years old." The headmistress, a slim woman, spoke in sincere tones.

"Not six, right?"

"Right. Only—"

"Only what?"

"With children it is very difficult to judge whether a death is suicide or not. There's rarely any suicide note, unlike with adults. And there are cases abroad of suicide at age six."

"However, in Japan, the youngest suicide on record was at age seven," insisted Tasaka. Statistics didn't lie, he reasoned with himself. According to the statistics in Japan, the youngest suicide on record was at age seven, so wasn't that proof that it was strange for a six-year-old to have killed himself?

One more to me, he thought as he left the kindergarten. One step at a time, he would track down the proof of murder: he repeated this over and over to himself as he walked through the slushy streets.

Later that night, however, on his way back to the home that lay empty with nobody waiting for him, his fervor gave way to a profound weariness. He himself did not know why. As he climbed the dark concrete staircase to his apartment, he even began to feel there was no point in hounding down Kyoko Igarashi. He shook his head lightly in confusion. Wouldn't it be just as futile as chasing after his own wife when she had left him?

Get a grip! Tasaka grimaced at himself. He already had the door key ready in his hand when he noticed with a start that there was a light on inside.

The door was unlocked, too. It was no laughing matter for a detective's home to be burgled. Bracing himself, he took a deep breath and opened the door, then stood rooted to the spot, stunned.

There, in the small room, was Misako, the wife who had walked out on him two years earlier.

She looked up at Tasaka with a tearful smile. "Welcome home," she said hoarsely.

Tasaka hastily shut the door. A savage feeling welled up in his chest. He wanted to hit her, hard. But instead he stared at her, his eyes cold. He did not restrain himself out of any kindness to her, but because he was scared that if he did hit her, he might end up forgiving her.

"Why are you here?" he asked still standing there, his voice emotionless. Misako wore heavy makeup, but beneath it he could see she was looking haggard.

"I want to apologize to you," she said. "Please forgive me."

"You're saying it to the wrong person, aren't you? What about that TV star beau of yours?"

"Don't talk about that man—"

"He dumped you, then?"

Tears welled up in Misako's trademark huge eyes. It was no exaggeration to say that Tasaka had been charmed by those beautiful eyes and had married her for them. He felt himself vacillate and chewed his lip.

"Do you think it serves me right?"

"Yeah," he said curtly. "Any reason I shouldn't?"

"No. Everyone thinks so," she said meekly, then looked around the room. "Where is she? Let me see Mika."

"Mika's not here."

"Not here?"

"She's dead."

"Dead?"

"Yes, dead." Tasaka felt the rage building up inside him all over again, and his voice turned rough. "Mika died the same day you ran off. By the time I got home from work, she was already dead. She went after you and fell in a gutter, and couldn't climb out again. She was only two! When I pulled her out, she was curled up like a fetus, dead. *You* killed her."

For a moment Misako stared into space, her eyes hollow. Then, all of a sudden, she collapsed in tears. Tasaka watched her back quivering, before abruptly storming out of the apartment and into the night.

He had no clear memory of where or how he had walked. When he returned to his apartment, still not in charge of himself, his legs were covered with mud up to his knees.

The light was still on inside. But there was no sign of Misako.

Ono was taken aback at Tasaka's appearance. His eyes were red and bloodshot, and he clearly had not had enough sleep.

"You're looking rough," he commented, worried. "Is the investigation going badly?"

"Not at all. I'll have conclusive evidence of murder within two or three days," Tasaka responded, his expression grim. Ono felt the defensive hunch of his shoulders belied his confidence.

"Hey, take it easy," he said, but Tasaka rushed out the door without replying.

Ono felt uneasy. Tasaka's attitude to this case had been abnormal from the start, and today it was excessively so. Had something happened last night?

This is looking bad, he thought. Just the fact that Tasaka was not pursuing Kyoko Igarashi purely out of a sense of justice was dangerous. If he went too far, it could prove fatal to him. *Wouldn't it be best to go after Tasaka and take him off the case?*

Ono was in two minds about it. He started to get up, but just then the telephone rang beside him. He picked it up.

"This is K—— Hospital. May I speak to Detective Tasaka?" A woman spoke urgently, her voice dry.

"Hospital?" echoed Ono, then added, "Detective Tasaka is out at present. May I ask what it's about?"

"Well, when he comes back, please tell him that his wife is in hospital. She attempted suicide."

"Attempted suicide?" Ono instantly recalled what he had heard from Detective Yokoi at Ueno police station. It must be the wife who had run off with that TV celebrity. But why on earth would she have tried to kill herself?

After hanging up, Ono tried to think where Tasaka might have gone, but he had no idea. Waiting impatiently for him to return, Ono began fretting about going to the hospital himself. He wanted to know what sort of woman Tasaka's wife was.

The hospital was in Aoyama. On the door of the third-floor room, there was a brand new name tag "Misako Tasaka."

When he opened the door and went in, a middle-aged nurse warned "Quietly!" in a low voice. "Are you her husband?"

"No, a friend," replied Ono.

Misako Tasaka lay with her eyes closed, asleep. It occurred to Ono that her pale face actually resembled that of Kyoko Igarashi.

According to the nurse, Misako had been found under a tree in the outer gardens of Meiji Jingu shrine, having taken an overdose of sleeping pills. She had been found quickly, so they had pumped her stomach and managed to save her life.

"A while ago she came to, and kept calling out her husband's name," added the nurse.

Ono sat with his arms folded, watching Misako sleep. There was no way that he, an outsider, could know why she had tried to kill herself. But he imagined that if things between Tasaka and her had gone well, then Tasaka would not be behaving like he was now. According to what Detective Yokoi had told him, she had left her husband and daughter, but to Ono's eyes she didn't look like that sort of woman at all. She looked very ordinary. Maybe it was because she was so ordinary that she had become infatuated?

Suddenly Misako opened her eyes wide. For a while she gazed at the ceiling, her eyes unfocused, but eventually she noticed Ono at her bedside and absently turned her gaze to him.

"Tasaka will be here soon," said Ono, looking closely at her. "My name is Ono, I work with him."

Misako just looked at Ono with her vacant eyes, apparently not yet completely recovered from the effect of the drug. From her expression he could tell that her consciousness was gradually becoming clearer.

"Did you meet Tasaka last night?" Ono said what was on his mind. It was the only reason he could think of to explain Tasaka's unnatural appearance this morning.

"Tasaka…" Her voice caught in her throat. "He won't forgive me!"

"You know, he's a kind man at heart," Ono smiled at her. He hoped he was right. Not for her sake, but for Tasaka's own sake. If Tasaka could forgive his wife, he would also probably be able to take a more tolerant, reasonable attitude towards Kyoko Igarashi. "I'll bring him here," he added, trying to set her mind at rest.

Meanwhile, Tasaka had at last caught up with Kyoko Igarashi in a restaurant in Ginza. She was with an overweight, middle-aged man, but as soon as Tasaka approached, the man rose slowly to his feet and left the restaurant.

Kyoko glared at Tasaka, her eyes fierce. "What do you want now?" Her voice shook. Her face was a blend of fury and scorn, but Tasaka also detected a note of fear. She was frightened. Indeed, having the truth exposed was scary.

"I just want you to tell me the truth," said Tasaka slowly, deliberately needling her. He lit up a cigarette.

"But I've already told you the truth!" Kyoko's voice became shrill.

Tasaka shook his head. "A six-year-old's suicide? Whoever would believe such a thing!"

"But it's true. You saw his suicide note yourself, didn't you?"

"Do you really expect the police to credit something like that?" Tasaka gave a snort of laughter. "I know what you did. That child had become a nuisance to you. A child of six is extremely gullible, especially with someone as close to him as his mother. No doubt you used that. If you just kept telling him that if he ate these pellets, he would be able to go to join his father in Heaven, a child of six would believe you, wouldn't he? Small children don't have any clear image of death. He would just believe that if he ate those pellets, he'd be able to meet his father."

"Are you saying that I killed my son?" Kyoko's lip quivered.

Tasaka slowly stubbed out his cigarette in the ashtray before asking, "Didn't you?"

"I shall instruct my lawyer to file a complaint against you. I will not tolerate you treating me like a murderer."

"Be my guest," said Tasaka curtly.

Kyoko rose to her feet with a clatter and ran out of the restaurant. The other customers and the waitresses stared after her in astonishment.

Instead of following her, Tasaka instead caught one of the waitresses and quizzed her about the man who had been with Kyoko.

"Actually, he's the boss of a real estate agency," the waitress told him. She could not say what kind of relationship Kyoko had with him, but Tasaka felt it would probably be worth meeting him.

Saijo Real Estate in Yotsuya was easy to find. It was not one of the usual small neighborhood offices plastered with ads, but a fine three-storied building.

Mr. Saijo looked at Tasaka, then commented with a smile, "We met a while ago in that restaurant in Ginza, didn't we?" When Tasaka mentioned Kyoko Igarashi's name, he said simply, "Yes, I know her well. A friend introduced me to her in a nightclub. I'm still single despite my age, so I was keen to get to know her."

"How close are you?"

"She asked me to marry her," he grinned. He seemed part proud, part bashful.

"Oh!" said Taguchi, his eyes wide. "And when was that?"

"A couple of weeks ago. She was more enamored of my fortune than of me personally, for sure. She's pretty hard up, it seems."

"Are you sure about that?"

"She told me herself. She didn't have much work, and with no money coming in, things were pretty tough."

"So what happened with the marriage talk?"

"I liked her, but the catch was that she had a child. I'm afraid I'm just not fond of kids. It's just the way I am, I guess."

"So you turned her down?"

"Well, not in so many words, but…"

"What was her reaction?"

"It seems it came as quite a shock to her. I think she'd expected me to jump at the chance."

"You know about her son's death, right?"

"Of course I do. It's all over the papers, for one thing."

"What did you think when you found out about it?"

"Well, it was right after I turned her down, so I did wonder whether she might have killed him because of me. But of course, I'm sure she couldn't have done that."

Tasaka was satisfied with Mr. Saijo's answer. He had found the motive for murder. Kyoko Igarashi had been in financial trouble and had wanted to marry the realtor Mr. Saijo, but her child stood in the way. Furthermore, the child in question had been more attached to his father, who had died in an accident, than he had been to her, his mother. This being so, she would not have felt such trauma at the idea of killing him. Parents are not always full of affection for their child. They can also be cruel to them.

Lost in thought, Tasaka recalled his own wife and grimaced. Misako had also abandoned her own two-year-old daughter, who was in the way, in order to shack up with some TV star, and because of that Mika had died. She and Kyoko Igarashi were really similar. No, they were the same, he decided.

Ono caught Tasaka on his return to Akasaka police station.

"Go straight to K—— Hospital," he told him. "Your wife attempted suicide."

"Misako?" Tasaka paled.

"That's right," Ono spoke forcefully. "She wants to see you. Go there now—the hospital in Aoyama."

"No, I won't."

"What do you mean, you won't?" Ono's voice was unusually sharp. "Why not?"

"I haven't got time. I have to go and see Kyoko Igarashi right away. I found the motive. She had a man interested in her and her son was in the way of them getting married. So she killed him. That's proof of murder," Tasaka replied without pausing for breath. His eyes shone. Ono felt it was more than the usual excitement at cornering a criminal. It was as if Tasaka was whipping himself into a frenzy.

"May I give you bit of advice?" asked Ono. Tasaka didn't say anything. "You should leave this case. Look, I'm worried about you. You're going to end up hurt. Forget about Kyoko Igarashi, and instead go along to the hospital. Your wife needs you."

"No. There's no way I can leave this case knowing that it's murder."

"Do you really believe it's murder? Aren't you just trying to convince yourself of it?"

"What are you trying to say?" Tasaka bristled.

Ono was not of a mind to back down. "You are hurling all the hatred you feel towards your wife onto Kyoko Igarashi, aren't you?" he said. "I have some idea of what went on between you and your wife. I understand why you're angry. But in the end it's your own personal problem. You should not be projecting it onto Kyoko Igarashi."

"Well I'm not."

"Are you sure of that?"

"Yes. This is a murder case. That's why I'm going after her."

"No. You're going into this case with your own preconceptions. If that's not so, then why are you so afraid?"

"Afraid? What the hell have I got to be afraid of?"

"That's why you won't go to the hospital. You're frightened you might end up forgiving your wife. And if you forgive your wife, you won't be able to pursue Kyoko Igarashi either. That's what you're afraid of."

"Don't be ridiculous."

"In that case, go and see your wife right away. She is full of regrets, and even tried to kill herself. Forgive her! There are times when, rather than being hard on people, it's necessary to show leniency. This is one of them."

"It's none of your business!" spat Tasaka. His face twitching, he turned his back and marched out of the room.

Ono sighed. His words had had the opposite effect of what he had intended, and he had ended up merely hardening Tasaka's resolve, he thought ruefully.

Attempted suicide, huh? muttered Tasaka to himself as he walked to NTV. Had Misako really intended to die, or had she just put on a charade thinking he would more easily forgive her?

Tasaka felt himself getting more and more worked up.

By the time he caught up with Kyoko Igarashi in the corridor of the TV station, he was in a rage. When she saw his face, she shrank back.

"Please, don't bother me anymore," she said, her voice tired.

Tasaka stood, blocking her way, and stared hard at her. "How about putting a stop to all these lies? You killed your child because he was in your way, didn't you?"

"What—"

"He was in the way of you getting married, so you killed him."

"That's nonsense!"

"Stop lying. I've investigated it thoroughly. You were in financial trouble, and asked that realtor to marry you. Isn't that true?"

"But—"

"But he passed on marrying a divorcée with a kid in tow. This is also a fact."

"B—"

"So you killed your son who was standing in your way."

"No, you're wrong! He killed himself!"

"Whoever's going to believe a six-year-old would kill himself? You had the motive. And you didn't even love the child. The day after he died you calmly took yourself off to work—that's proof enough. You killed him!"

"It's a lie! A lie!" she screamed hysterically. Just at that moment, there was a sudden bright flash to one side of them. Two young paparazzi were there.

"Ah!" exclaimed Kyoko, covering her face with her hands. The reporters ran off, excitement glowing on their faces.

"That's really gone and done it!" she groaned, leaning shakily against the wall. "You've ruined my life. Have you any idea what you've done? Tomorrow, the rumor that I am a cruel mother who killed her child will have spread all over Japan. I finally became a star only to be dragged down again."

"That's what happens when you commit murder."

"Murder?"

"That's right. You killed your child."

"Ah, so I did. I killed my son. I'm an evil, bloodsucking monster. Now are you satisfied?" Kyoko Igarashi suddenly shrieked with laughter.

The next day, there it was in the society pages of the morning paper: "Kyoko Igarashi suspected of murder." The headline was small, but the report stated that the police were investigating the actress on suspicion of having murdered the son she claimed had committed suicide. In the same section, there was an even briefer report that Misako Tasaka had attempted suicide.

Ono read both reports with mixed feelings. Tasaka had finally driven Kyoko Igarashi into a corner. Ono had no idea what would happen next. What he did know was that Tasaka was in a dangerous fix.

Ono glanced over at Tasaka. He too was reading the paper, but before long he threw it down, got to his feet, and left the room.

Is he going to the hospital? Ono hoped he was. He followed him out, but the taxi he hailed outside the police station was headed in the opposite direction from the hospital.

He was evidently on his way to further harass Kyoko Igarashi. In other words, he was driving himself into an even tighter corner.

That night, what Ono had feared would happen, did happen.

Called in to see the Chief, he was immediately aware of a tense atmosphere in the room. The Chief was normally seated, his bulk squeezed into his swivel chair, but today he was pacing restlessly around the room.

"Detective Tasaka not back yet?" he queried, still pacing.

"Not yet."

"I don't suppose you know where he went?"

"I think he's probably out there investigating that case."

"Go find him and bring him here."

"Has something happened?"

"Kyoko Igarashi has committed suicide. She gassed herself. There was a call from the local station."

"Suicide?" Ono felt a chill run down his spine.

The Chief stopped pacing and looked sourly at Ono. "Unfortunately, she left a suicide note complaining about the police. Her lawyer held a press conference and read it out to the assembled reporters."

"That's bad."

"It's more than bad," the Chief's raised his voice. "By tomorrow, the entire media will be attacking the police. Did Detective Tasaka find his proof?"

"He said he found the motive."

"A motive's no good without evidence. You know that."

"Isn't it possible Kyoko Igarashi killed herself because she realized there was no escape?"

"I wouldn't try consoling yourself with that if I were you."

Ono didn't answer. He himself knew it was a hollow comfort. After all, Kyoko Igarashi had left a suicide note laying the blame squarely on the police. And now that Kyoko was dead it would be difficult to pin anything on her.

"I think I'd better put Detective Tasaka on leave for a while," said the Chief weakly.

Tasaka walked along in the rain, weighed down by a sense of defeat.

Kyoko Igarashi's suicide had been widely reported on TV. The reports stated that she had been cornered into suicide after the TV drama she was working on was cancelled once it became known that the police suspected her of murder. It was rich for the TV station that had cancelled the drama to place all the blame on the police, but it couldn't be helped.

The Chief had told him to take a break. It had sounded like a declaration of Tasaka's failure.

He still believed Kyoko Igarashi had killed her son. Now that she had also killed herself, however, there was no possibility of pursuing it further. He knew very well that everyone would stand up for her and censure the police.

Her lawyer had lodged an official complaint; Tasaka had gone from being the accuser to being the accused.

Tasaka felt his resolve weakening.

Before he knew it, he found his legs taking him in the direction of K—— Hospital. On the way he stopped at a florist and bought a small bunch of flowers—the first in two years.

By the time he arrived at the hospital, he was soaked through from the rain. He asked at reception which room Misako Tasaka was in.

The young nurse looked at Tasaka with sleepy eyes. "That patient has already been discharged," she said drowsily.

"Where has she gone?"

"How should I know?"

"Oh…" said Tasaka vacantly, and walked listlessly back out into the rain.

The flowers were left behind, forgotten, in the hospital.